Cinderella's Sweet-Talking Marine

CATHIE LINZ

CENTER POINT PUBLISHING
THORNDIKE, MAINE

This Center Point Large Print edition
is published in the year 2005 by arrangement with
Harlequin Enterprises Ltd.

Copyright © 2004 by Cathie L. Baumgardner.

The text of this Large Print edition is unabridged. In other
aspects, this book may vary from the original edition. Printed in
Thailand. Set in 16-point Times New Roman type.

ISBN 1-58547-564-5

Library of Congress Cataloging-in-Publication Data

Linz, Cathie.
    Cinderella's sweet-talking marine / Cathie Linz.--Center Point large print ed.
        p. cm.
    ISBN 1-58547-564-5 (lib. bdg. : alk. paper)
        1. United States. Marine Corps--Fiction. 2. Mothers and daughters--Fiction.
    3. Single mothers--Fiction. 4. Large type books. I. Title.

PS3562.I558C56 2005
813'.54--dc22

2004020456

Chapter One

Ben Kozlowski was a Marine with money. But it hadn't made him a happy man. The inheritance from his wealthy oilman grandfather had made him feel somewhat guilty when he'd first heard about it. After all, he'd done nothing to deserve it.

But that guilt was nothing compared to the guilt that had driven him into this honky-tonk just off the North Carolina Interstate, in a town called Pine Hills. He wasn't there to drown his sorrows in the bottom of a bottle of whiskey, tempting as that might sound. No, he was here looking for a woman.

And not just any woman. He was here to find Ellie Jensen.

A neighbor at her apartment building said she was at work and had given him the name of this place.

Ben had been in plenty of bars during the course of his adult life, from cantinas in South America to exotic dives in Asia. Each had their own unique smell blended with the customary tobacco smoke. This particular place seemed to specialize in the scent of burnt onions. A big chalkboard on the wall proclaimed that Al's Place made burgers the way you wanted them—hot and juicy. And apparently dripping with onions.

The place was crowded, with country music blaring from a jukebox in the corner. Guys wearing jeans and T-shirts pressed their beer bellies against the bar, barely able to fit onto the stools provided. They sported a variety of baseball caps advertising various brands of their favorite malt liquor beverage.

The rest of the room had booths around the perimeter and tables placed wherever they'd fit, not leaving much room for the servers to get by.

Which seemed to suit the clientele just fine.

Ben could understand the appeal. The females—and *all* the servers were female—were dressed in short, tight denim skirts and skimpy tank tops. The closer the servers got, the easier it was for the customers to cop a feel.

Ben tugged out the well-worn photo and fingered the sweet face displayed there. John Riley had been one of Ben's closest friends and Ellie was John's sister, his only family.

Take care of my sister. Promise me you'll take care of my sister. Ben had held John in his arms as he lay mortally wounded by friendly fire and he'd sworn he'd take care of his friend's sister.

So here he was.

And there she was. He spotted her across the smoke-filled room. She was struggling to balance a tray filled with heavy beer mugs while avoiding the unwanted advances of a customer.

Ben was at her side a second later. "Let the lady go."

His tone of voice, that of a Marine who meant business, got the customer's attention despite the fact that he'd had a few too many brews. But it didn't make him obey the order. "Who're you?" the guy slurred.

"I'm the man who's going to make you sorry you were born if you don't let her go right now."

This time the guy not only paid attention, he obeyed.

Holding up his hands in the international signal of surrender, he said, "Hey bud, I didn't mean nothing by it."

Ben ignored the man and instead focused his attention on Ellie. She'd hurried on to another table, depositing the beers as quickly as she could before returning to the bar for another order.

She had incredibly long legs and a graceful way of moving. Her dark hair was pinned up as if she'd tried to get it out of her way, but one strand had come undone, drawing his attention to her nape. Her skin was creamy pale, not tanned. The line of her back was as rigidly upright as that of any private in the Marine Corps standing at attention.

She clearly didn't belong in a place like this. So what was she doing working here?

Ellie was aware of the man staring at her. She'd noticed him the moment he'd walked in. He was that kind of guy. The kind you noticed. He had dark hair and was alarmingly handsome with light hazel eyes that caught her attention even from across the smoky room.

She also was aware that, given his short haircut, he was probably military. Which would explain his lean but muscular build and the tense and dangerous aura he projected. Camp Lejeune, one of the major Marine training bases, was almost an hour away. Not right in their backyard, but close enough to get an occasional visitor.

Ellie was grateful that the stranger rescued her from the huge bear of a drunk who'd been pawing her. But that didn't mean that she was looking to start anything with this newcomer. Gratitude only went so far, and she'd learned early on that it didn't pay to count on anyone but yourself.

She'd forgotten that lesson when she'd fallen in love with her ex-husband, Perry Jensen. She'd let him sweep her off her feet with his sweet-talking, charming ways. No good had come of it, except for her daughter, Amy. Amy was the reason for Ellie to get up in the morning.

That was especially true now that Ellie's brother, Johnny, was dead. She still couldn't believe that he was gone. She liked to think that he was still serving the Marines someplace overseas. But the arrival of the representative of the Marine Corps had been all too real when he'd told her the news of Johnny's death, and conveyed the appreciation of a nation and the regret of the entire Corps.

Friendly fire. Under investigation. She'd only registered part of what the uniformed representative had said six weeks ago. Johnny had been buried with full military honors. She'd been given a folded flag as an official remembrance.

But Ellie couldn't think about that now. She had a job to do. She couldn't afford to give the manager of this dive any excuse to fire her. She needed the money.

The newcomer was still staring at her. She could feel his eyes on her, but his gaze didn't have the smarmy feel of so many of the others. He wore jeans and a black T-shirt, which was common enough attire in this part of the country. But he wore them with a confidence that stood out. *He* stood out.

And he was walking toward her.

Great. Now she'd have to deal with him. Well, better

to confront before being confronted. Keeping her smile cool and her voice equally so, she said, "Thanks again for your help."

"I need to talk to you."

Yeah, right. How many times had she heard that line since she'd started waitressing. *Come on, honey, sit down and talk to me.* "Sorry, but I'm very busy right now."

"Ellie," he began when she interrupted him.

"How do you know my name?"

"Can we go someplace to talk?"

"No." The intense way he was looking at her made her nervous.

"I'm not here to hurt you. I've come to help."

Yeah, right. "As I said, I'm busy right now."

"This man bothering you?" Earl, the burly bartender, demanded. A professional wrestler in a previous life, Earl's smooth head was as buffed as his muscular arms.

The newcomer didn't appear the least bit intimidated. "Where were you when that drunk customer was bothering her?" he demanded of Earl.

"Serving drinks, that's where I was. I may have missed that action but I can still take you out if I have to."

"There's no need for that," Ellie said, putting her hand on Earl's beefy arm, just above the barbed wire tattoo and below the one of a bulldog.

"Former Marine?" the newcomer asked Earl who nodded.

The newcomer then lifted the cuff on his T-shirt to show his own bulldog tattoo.

"Ooh-rah!" Earl shouted, startling Ellie and half the guys at the bar.

"Ooh-rah!" the newcomer repeated, just as intensely if not as loudly before slapping Earl's outstretched hand in a high five. "Captain Ben Kozlowski," he said to Earl. "Do you mind if I talk to Ellie here for a few minutes? It's official business."

Her heart stopped. "Is it Johnny? Did they make a mistake? Is he still alive?"

She vaguely saw Ben shake his head before the entire room telescoped and went black.

Ben caught Ellie before she collapsed onto the floor. Sweeping her up into his arms, he followed Earl's hurried directions to the employee's exit and the fresh air outside. A rush of warmth hit him, rising from the pavement.

Although it was only early March, the temperature was already in the low eighties today. The bright sunlight highlighted Ellie's pale face. She felt so fragile as he carried her.

Ben cursed himself for not having handled things better. But his track record in that department lately was pretty abysmal. He hadn't been doing much right lately. He wasn't here on any official business of the Marine Corps, he was here to honor his buddy's dying wishes.

Heading for his Bronco, Ben shifted her in his arms as he opened the passenger door and gently set her on the seat before reaching for the bottle of water he had nearby. Keeping one arm around her, he dabbed some water on a paper towel he ripped from a roll behind the driver's seat. Before placing the dampened cloth on her forehead, he felt her neck to check her pulse. Her skin was so soft beneath his fingertips.

"Get your hands off me!" She shoved him away with surprising strength and he narrowly avoided hitting the back of his head on the dashboard.

"Take it easy," he said in a soothing voice, holding his hands up as the guy had in the bar earlier. "I'm not going to hurt you."

She knew better. He'd already hurt her just by being here. And he'd angered her by showing up at her place of employment. She felt like an idiot for passing out the way she had, even if it had only been for a moment. She glared at him. She'd displayed weakness, something she hated, and it was all his fault. Reason alone to want him gone. "Since when do the Marines send someone out of uniform to do anything official? I'm not buying that story for one minute. So you'd better start talking, Captain, and you'd better start talking fast or I'll have Earl take care of you." Her words reflected her fury. "What kind of idiot walks into a bar and tells a woman who's recently lost her brother what you told me?"

"Let's start over, shall we? My name is Ben Kozlowski. I knew your brother. He was a close buddy of mine."

"How close? Were you there when he died?"

Ben nodded.

"Then why didn't you do something to save him?"

His gut clenched. Her unsteady question wasn't one he hadn't asked himself a thousand times ever since that awful moment. He'd give anything to have changed the way things had happened.

"I'm sorry."

"Sorry won't bring him back."

"I realize that."

Her gaze turned suspicious. "You weren't the one who shot him, were you?"

"No, I wasn't the one who shot him." But he might as well have been. Not that he could tell her that. He wasn't here to try and clear his conscience. He was here to make good on a promise. A vow.

So Ben slammed the hatch on his own turbulent emotions, and concentrated on Ellie. She was clearly displeased with him and he couldn't blame her. He hadn't handled things very well so far.

She was still pale, but she was no weak victim. There was nothing submissive about the tilt of her chin.

He was watching her again. She felt his gaze on her. She met it head-on. She wasn't going to back away. "Johnny wrote me about you." She fiercely tried to keep her voice steady. She'd already made a big enough fool of herself by fainting like that. And then by spurning his apology, asking him if he'd shot her brother. She was a mess. Not like her. She had to get her act together. She hadn't had time to eat that day. Low blood sugar, that's why she'd passed out. She gathered her thoughts. "You weren't at his funeral, though."

"I'm sorry I couldn't make it. I was still overseas."

"Is that why you tracked me down? To offer your condolences?"

"I wanted to check up on you."

"I appreciate the thought," she said stiffly, clearly

indicating that she didn't really appreciate it at all. "But there's no need."

"I think there's every need. You don't belong in a place like this." He jerked his head toward the bar.

"I can take care of myself."

"It didn't look that way to me."

She tugged on the skimpy hem of her skirt before replying. "I don't need you walking into my life and telling me what to do. What I do need is to get back to work."

"You just fainted!"

"Because you scared me by saying you were here on official business about Johnny." It was idiotic of her to think that the military had made a mistake. She'd stood by the grave site. Seen his casket lowered into the ground. But she'd had a vivid dream the night before where her brother, with that crooked grin of his, had told her that his death was a big mistake.

"I'm sorry, I shouldn't have put it that way."

"Yeah, well . . ." She swung her long legs out the open car door, dislodging him in the process.

Standing, he held out his hand to assist her, but she didn't take his offer of help, preferring to do it herself.

She was taller than he'd thought at first, the top of her head reaching to just beneath his chin. He reached out to smooth the tendrils of dark hair that had fallen across her pale face.

"When was the last time you ate?" he demanded.

"I'm fine," she insisted, backing up to glare at him.

"You're not pregnant, are you? Is that why you fainted?"

"No, I'm not pregnant," she said, highly offended.

"Look, I'm just trying to figure out what's going on with you."

"What's going on is that you are beginning to irritate me," Ellie retorted. "What gives you the right to walk in here out of the blue and start interrogating me as if I were one of your Marines? I'm not. I'm the responsible mother of a five-year-old. I can handle anything." She prayed that if she kept saying that often enough, she'd start believing it eventually.

Maybe she could handle anything, but Ben knew he couldn't. He couldn't handle the fact that she was swaying on her feet from exhaustion, that she was clearly struggling to make ends meet. "Why do you work here? I thought John told me you were waitressing in a nice family restaurant, some sort of mom-and-pop place."

"I was, but it went bankrupt suddenly a few months ago. This was the only job I could get. I don't have a college degree." She'd left school to work, to support Perry who was getting his degree. Yet another example of how love had blinded her and made her stupid. "I didn't want my brother worrying about me so I didn't tell him about my new job. Which reminds me, how did you find me?"

"I had your address. From John. You weren't there, but a neighbor told me you worked here." He waved his hand toward Al's Place in a dismissive move. "Let me help you. I can give you some money until things settle down."

"I can't take money from you." What kind of woman

did he think she was? "I don't need any handouts."

"John would want me to help you and he'd want you to accept that help."

His words hit a nerve. "Don't you dare tell me what my brother would want!" she said fiercely. "I knew him better than you did. We grew up together. Being bounced from foster home to foster home, we only had each other to count on. I knew my brother my entire life. All twenty-five years of it. And now he's gone. So don't you try and make me do what you want by using my brother's name."

She didn't even realize she'd been jabbing her finger at Ben's chest until he cradled her hand in his. "I'm sorry. I shouldn't have said that. I seem to be messing up a lot today."

He was certainly messing up her self-control. First fainting like that, and then going ballistic on him.

And now, with his fingers enclosing hers, she felt something new—the stirring of attraction. Her unexpected reaction threw her. The aching need to be held, to be comforted, to be loved threatened to overwhelm her.

Her startled gaze met his. This close to him she could see flecks of green in his hazel eyes, could see the laugh lines at the corners of his eyes, could see a faint scar along the right line of his jaw.

The warmth from his fingers sent treacherous longings through her. It had been so long since she'd felt this powerful tug, this whirlpool of dangerously seductive sensations.

She couldn't give in. She had to be strong.

But that was hard to do given the fact that her emotions had been dangerously close to the surface ever since her brother's death. More and more she felt as if she were being buried alive beneath a pile of problems too insurmountable to overcome.

She knew she couldn't give in, she knew she couldn't give up. She had Amy to think of.

Just thinking about her little girl gave Ellie strength. Amy was the best kid on the face of the earth. And Perry was the scum of the earth for not realizing that and cherishing and protecting his little girl, instead of abandoning them when he found out two years ago that Amy had asthma.

No, Ellie, had to be strong, not just for herself but for Amy. She couldn't be distracted by sexual chemistry.

Belatedly tugging her hand from Ben's, she repeated her earlier statement. "I have to get back to work."

"Why won't you let me help you?"

Because then I might become dependent on that help and when you leave, the situation would just get worse. Been there, done that. Aloud, she said, "Because, it's best that I stand on my own two feet."

"So you're telling me that you have so many friends, that you can't use another one? You can depend on me, Ellie. I didn't just track you down to say hi, and then walk away. I'm here for the long-term."

"You're a Marine, Ben. You don't stay anywhere long-term. Your life belongs to the Corps."

"I've got a new deployment relatively nearby, at Camp Lejeune. So I will be nearby. You're not getting rid of me that easily."

His smile was charming, his tone of voice encouraging. But she'd heard it before. Perry telling her she could count on him, that he'd always be there for her. Talk was cheap.

No, she had to be strong, she had to rely on herself only.

As if to prove that he was just as determined as she was, Ben stayed at Al's Place until her shift was over. He held the door open for her as she left, and insisted on walking her to her car, which looked like it was held together with baling wire.

The ten-year-old Toyota certainly wouldn't win any beauty contests—not with its multicolored body, a majority of which was green, except for the passenger doors which were silver. A friend of a friend knew someone who did cheap body work, and when someone had slammed into her car while it was parked in the supermarket lot, she didn't have the money to get it fixed. Contacting her auto insurance company was out of the question because that would only raise her premiums, which she barely scraped out now.

"How many miles do you have on this thing?" Ben asked, as if suspicious it couldn't go another mile without falling apart.

There were mornings when it refused to turn over that she wondered the same thing. "The odometer stopped working at 199,999 miles. It may not look pretty but it gets me from point A to point B."

"Are you headed straight home?"

She nodded. She was too tired to argue with him anymore.

"What about dinner?"

"What about it?" she countered.

"Would you and your daughter join me for dinner tonight? My treat. I hear there's a great steak house near here."

Being strong only went so far. She was down to her last package of macaroni and cheese and one oversized generic-brand can of green beans, which was what they'd had for dinner last night.

Tomorrow was payday so she'd be able buy more food then. But tonight . . .

Steak? When was the last time she'd had steak?

What was the harm in going out with Ben just this once? Amy would get a good dinner. Surely it wouldn't hurt.

What would hurt would be to believe that Ben would still be here a week from now, or two weeks. To believe his charming words, to fall for his sexy good looks. That would be a huge mistake. One the formerly weak Ellie might have made when she still believed in happily-ever-after.

But the new Ellie knew better. No matter how good his hands had felt on her, no matter how seductive the chemistry might be, the only thing she could count on was that Ellie had to take care of Ellie. And take care of her daughter.

That was the bottom line, that was where her focus was and would remain . . . no matter how attractive Captain Ben Kozlowski was.

Chapter Two

"So what do you say?" Ben's voice was coaxing. "How about dinner? Will you and your daughter join me?"

Ellie was tempted, *so* tempted. She wavered. Macaroni and green beans again for dinner . . . or steak. Saying yes didn't have to mean giving in. It didn't have to mean that she was weak. It could mean that she was being strong enough to look at this situation realistically, objectively. Having one dinner with Ben was not going to change her, wasn't going to make her a believer in happily-ever-afters.

"Come on. I could really use the company."

He made it seem like *he* was the needy one. She wondered if that was a deliberate tactic on his part. Trying to make it seem as if she'd be doing him a favor by saying yes instead of making it seem like he was taking pity on a charity case.

Which would make Ben more empathetic than she'd expected. But then there had to be something okay about Ben if her brother had liked him. Johnny had been a pretty good judge of character most of the time. Like her, he didn't trust easily. But he'd trusted Ben.

Thinking about Johnny hurt so much. But Ellie refused to show it. She'd played a weepy wimp enough for one day. It wasn't a customary role for her. She'd had to be tough to survive the foster care system and not let it grind her up. Being tough included learning how to keep her emotions under wraps, how to hide her pain.

Ellie had few vulnerabilities. Her brother and her daughter. That was it.

And now her brother was gone. Which meant Ellie had to work even harder to do the right thing for Amy. Ellie's stomach growled, reminding her that she had to take care of herself or she wouldn't be any use to Amy. "Okay. I accept your invitation."

Ben smiled. "Outstanding. I'll follow you home and then we can leave from there." Standing beside his big burly black Bronco, he stared at her means of transportation with distrust.

But Tiny the Toyota had always been there for her. She'd had the car since she was in college when she'd bought it used. Her husband had come and gone, but her trusty vehicle was still with her. Ready to take her wherever she needed to go, provided it wasn't too far. Capable of holding groceries, of moving furniture, of playing loud music from the radio that still worked on at least three stations. Dependable, reliable . . . okay, sometimes a little temperamental.

Unfortunately this was one of those times Tiny decided to be difficult. Muttering under her breath, Ellie yanked on the hood release and hopped out of the vehicle to lift the hood and jiggle a wire.

"What are you doing?" Ben was at her side.

"Working magic."

He could believe that. She'd already worked magic on him. She wasn't anything like he'd pictured. He'd imagined a sweet young woman. Sure, she had a child, so he knew she wasn't innocent. He just hadn't expected her to have a will of steel. And a basic knowledge of the workings of a car. He'd never met a woman who popped the hood on her car and went to work on it herself.

"That should do it." Ellie was startled when Ben lowered the hood for her as if she were a delicate flower. She wasn't accustomed to being looked after. Her ex-husband had opened doors for her and pulled out chairs when he'd been courting her, but had stopped after they were married. It hadn't happened overnight, but had been more of a gradual thing.

Ellie took a deep breath and kicked Perry out of her thoughts. She needed to stay focused on the here and now. Thankfully, Tiny behaved this time and obediently started up. There were no further exhibits of the car's temperamental nature on the short drive home.

The two-story brick apartment building didn't look like much from the outside, but it was across the street from a small park. It also had hardwood floors in the living room and two bedrooms, which made things easier with Amy's asthma. And it had Frenchie Sanchez.

In her early sixties, Frenchie didn't look like anyone's idea of a grandmother. She wasn't tall and willowy, but she moved as if she were. She was proud of the relatively few wrinkles on her face. She had short cropped hair which she frequently dyed when she got bored. Last month she'd been a platinum blonde, now she was a redhead. She had brown eyes, a loud laugh and a fondness for huge earrings. She wore flowing dresses and pants in colors like papaya and lime.

Frenchie attributed her colorful appearance to marrying a Cuban trumpet player in the early fifties and then moving with him to Europe. She had a Parisian woman's flair for scarves and a dancer's graceful confidence. She also had a heart of gold.

Ellie knew how extraordinarily lucky she was to have a neighbor like Frenchie to help out with Amy, to watch her while Ellie was at work. Frenchie resisted taking any money from Ellie, saying that Amy was wonderful company for her and prevented her from getting lonely. But Ellie had insisted, and had paid her what she could, which wasn't anything near what the older woman was worth. But then Frenchie Sanchez was priceless.

She greeted Ellie with her customary wide smile. "How was work today, *ma chère?*"

"Mommy, Mommy, look what I drewed!" Amy waved a piece of paper at her. At five, she was small for her age. She had Ellie's dark hair and brown eyes. Today she was wearing one of her favorite shorts sets, the T-shirt with a cat's face complete with rhinestone eyes.

Gazing down at her, Ellie felt her heart expand with emotion. It didn't seem like that long ago when she'd given birth and held a newborn Amy in her arms, marveling at her perfectly formed tiny fingers and nails, awed by the intensity of her love for her child.

Where had the time gone? Her baby had become a little girl. She knew it, but every so often it hit her again. Her daughter would only be small a short time, and Ellie hated missing a moment of the new discoveries to be had at this age.

"Let me see." Ellie bent down to hug her before

looking at the artwork. "That's a beautiful drawing."

"It's a cat."

"I can see that." Well, she couldn't really. It looked like a circle with eyeballs to Ellie. But because her little girl drew it, it was beautiful.

"Who's he?" Amy pointed at Ben.

Ellie had been so distracted that she'd forgotten to make the introductions. "He's a friend of Uncle Johnny's. His name is Ben."

"Uncle Johnny is in heaven now." Amy pointed skyward.

Ellie's throat tightened. "That's right."

"Are you from heaven?" Amy asked Ben.

"I'm from the Marines."

"So you're not an angel?"

"No."

"That's too bad. I thought you could take a message to my Uncle Johnny for me. And show him my drawing."

"I wish I could."

Ellie noted the strained expression on Ben's face.

Frenchie helped ease the moment with her usual skill. "Welcome to my home, Ben. Can I get you something to drink?"

"No, thank you, ma'am."

"Call me Frenchie. All my friends do. I got the nickname from all those years of living in Paris with my musician husband."

"It's a pleasure to meet you, Frenchie." Ben's voice had regained its customary tone. It sounded deep and very male.

Ellie looked down at her daughter, smoothing her hair away from her forehead. "Honey, Ben has invited us out to dinner tonight."

"So we don't have to eat beans again tonight? Yeah!" Amy quickly gathered her backpack. "I'm ready now."

"We have to go home so I can change out of my work clothes," Ellie reminded her, hoping her blush wasn't too obvious. Amy's enthusiasm made it seem as if she'd been eating beans for a month.

"Okay, but change fast, 'kay, Mommy? Are we going to have a Happy Meal?"

A meal at a fast-food place was a special treat as far as Amy was concerned. "No, we're going someplace even better."

"I didn't know there was any place better."

"Would you like to join us, Frenchie?" Ben asked the older woman.

"How sweet of you to invite me, but no thank you. The cable station is running an Antonio Banderas movie marathon. I can't miss that."

Ellie hugged her. "Thanks again for taking care of Amy, Frenchie."

"It's nothing, *ma chère*. Enjoy your evening out. You deserve it."

Amy raced across the hall to the door to their second-story apartment. Ben picked up her backpack and held the door open for Ellie after she'd unlocked and opened it.

"I . . . uh, I'll just be a minute or two. You're welcome to sit down and watch TV while I change." She gestured toward the couch and tried not to imagine how the place looked to Ben. Not that Marines were that interested in interior decorating. But he probably noticed that there wasn't much furniture. "I won't be long. Come on, Amy."

Ellie had her daughter sit on her bed with one of her favorite books. Then Ellie grabbed some clean clothes from her own bedroom before returning to the bathroom. The tobacco smoke that clung to Ellie's skin and hair as a result of working at Al's wasn't good for Amy. It wasn't particularly good for Ellie either, but her requests for a larger no-smoking area had resulted in her boss laughing at her.

Ellie rinsed off the bargain shampoo and turned off the faucet before reaching for a towel. She used the hair blower for about three minutes before turning it off and quickly braiding her still-damp hair into a single braid.

It didn't take her long to get dressed in the clothes she'd grabbed. Her wardrobe choices were extremely limited. She couldn't remember the last time she'd bought new clothes. Any extra money was spent on getting things for Amy. Which was fine by her. That was as it should be in her book.

Ellie tugged on a pair of black capri pants and a red knit top. She stuck her feet into the pair of sandals she'd picked up for a song at a discount store in the after-season sales a year or two ago.

A quick check in the bathroom mirror told her that she looked clean and respectable. Good. That's what she was aiming for. She added just a tad of makeup—a quick swipe of some eyeshadow and lipstick and then she was ready.

"Mommy, are you done yet?" Amy demanded from right outside the door.

"All ready." Ellie stepped out of the bathroom.

Looking over from the sports segment on the TV, Ben immediately rose to his feet. "You look nice."

Ben figured his words sounded lame, because the truth was that Ellie looked better than nice. And she smelled like fresh lemons. He got a whiff as she walked past him to get her jacket and purse from a hook near the front door.

"Allow me." He took the denim jacket from her hands and held it for her to slide her arms into.

She shot him a startled glance over her shoulder.

"Mommy, why do you need help getting dressed? I thought you knew how."

"I do know how. Ben is just being polite." She quickly reached back but had trouble finding the arm-holes. Her fingers bumped against the side of his leg. "Sorry about that." Now he'd think she was an idiot who couldn't even get a jacket on properly.

"No problem." He moved closer to smoothly guide her into the jacket. His hands rested on her shoulders for a moment. She felt his fingers brush against her bare skin as he lifted her braid from beneath the denim. Awareness streaked through her entire body starting at the contact point at her nape, racing down her spine and curling her toes. "There. How's that?"

How was it? Entirely too provocative. She was supposed to be keeping her objectivity here. Not melting.

Ellie didn't relax until they were seated at a table in the steak house. Amy was gazing at the children's menu as if she were able to read every word. She'd brought two dolls with her and she had them gazing at the menu with equal intentness.

"Do you want the chicken fingers?" Ellie asked Amy. Luckily her daughter didn't suffer from serious food allergies the way a lot of children with asthma did.

"I want octypuss," Amy proudly declared.

Ellie blinked. "What?" There were times when her child said things that came completely from another planet and this was one of them.

"Octypuss."

"They don't serve octopus here."

"Frenchie told me she ate some in Paris."

"When you're as old as Frenchie then you can have octopus."

Amy's face scrunched up. "I'll be two hundred by then."

Ellie tried not to laugh. "No, you won't. Now do you want chicken fingers or a hot dog?" Maybe a steak house wasn't that different from a fast-food place, from a kid's point of view.

"Chicken fingers. But no beans. No beans, Mommy. I don't like broccoli either. Remember?"

"Yes, I remember."

After they'd placed their orders, Amy eagerly leaned forward toward Ben. "Do you want to play with my Barbie? I've got two." She offered him one.

Ben didn't have the heart to tell the kid no.

"My Barbie works at the hops-ital," Amy declared. "Where does your Barbie work?"

"She's a Marine."

27

"What does she wear?"

"A uniform."

"Is she going to end up in heaven like my Uncle Johnny?"

His gut clenched. "Not until she's old and gray."

"Can she work at the hops-ital with my Barbie?"

"Sure."

"Okay, then. You go first." When he looked at a total loss, the little girl added, "Your Barbie talks to my Barbie."

"Hello."

Amy frowned. "You have to make her sound more like a girl."

"Hello." His voice rose to a higher pitch.

"What's your name?"

"Barbie."

"My name is Barbie, too. Let's have lunch." Amy sat her Barbie down at the table. "Do you have a pancake maker?"

"No."

"There's no mess. No mess at all. Amazing."

Ellie felt compelled to explain. "She saw an infomercial on the TV early one morning last week and it's stuck in her mind like glue."

"The pancakes don't taste like glue," Amy said. "And there's no mess. We don't like mess. Mess can make my asthma bad. Does your Barbie have asthma?"

"I don't know."

"You should see a doctor. Some doctors can be nice." Amy carefully rearranged her doll's sundress. "My Barbie is a doctor. That's why she works at the hops-ital. Okay, now let's go for a drive. My Barbie drives, yours just rides along." She kept up a constant monologue, meaning that Ben only had to say an occasional high-pitched "Yes," or "No."

"Captain Kozlowski?"

Ben looked up to find a fellow Marine and his wife staring at him as if he'd grown two heads. Ben dropped the Barbie like a hot potato and instantly rose to his feet.

"I didn't expect to see you here, sir," Gunnery Sergeant Handley said.

To which Ben replied, "I'm here with friends."

"I won't keep you then. Nice seeing you, sir."

Ben nodded briskly and waited until the Marine and his wife were some distance away and out of his sight line before sitting down again.

"You should have seen the expression on your face." Ellie shook her head. "It really was priceless."

"I'm so glad I could provide the comedic entertainment for our meal this evening," Ben drawled.

"What's com-dick entertainment?" Amy demanded.

"Comedic means funny," Ellie replied.

"I can be funny. I can make funny faces. Want to see?" She rolled her eyes and scrunched up her nose.

"Here's your dinner." Ellie moved the Barbies off the table and Amy put them on her lap.

The meal went well and Ellie ate every speck of her huge steak, baked potato and fresh grilled vegetables. Amy ate most of her meal and didn't insist on feeding her Barbies.

"What about some dessert?" their peppy waitress

inquired as she cleared their table of the empty plates. "Our specialty is Decadent Chocolate Delight."

"Sounds good," Ben said.

When the waitress brought the huge layered dessert, Amy's eyes almost bugged out. "Can I have the cherry on top?"

"Affirmative," Ben said.

Amy frowned. "What's that mean?"

"It means yes."

"What do you say?" Ellie prompted her as Ben handed Amy the juicy red cherry.

"Thank you, Ben." Amy gave him an ear-to-ear smile before leaning her head against his arm. "I like you."

His heart gave a funny thump and Ben knew he was a goner. He'd always been a sucker for those in need. He'd been that way since he was a kid and had seen a frightened kitten in the grocery store parking lot. A bunch of bigger kids had been trying to poke sticks at it as it frantically crouched under the Dumpster. Ben had fought them off and had rescued the kitten, bringing it home under his coat. He could still remember the way the little thing had stopped trembling and rested its head against his chest.

Oh, yeah, he'd always had a thing for rescuing the underdog . . . or kitten. For helping the smaller or weaker inhabitants on this planet.

Seeing Amy gazing at him with such appreciation at such a little thing as giving her a cherry brought out all his protective instincts. One dinner and already the kid had him in the palm of her hand.

Ellie noted the strange expression on Ben's face and

30

wondered at the reason for it. She'd been impressed by his ability to recover from his embarrassment at being found playing with dolls by one of his fellow Marines. He'd been incredibly good with Amy all evening.

That didn't mean that Ellie should depend on him for anything other than his temporary company. If only she could get a little more on her feet financially, then they'd be out of the woods.

On her way out, Ellie discreetly checked to see if the steak house was hiring any more servers, but they weren't.

The drive back home was uneventful. "Can Ben stay?" Amy asked as they neared their front door.

"It's already past your bedtime."

"I want Ben to tell me a bedtime story." Amy tugged him into the apartment with her, taking him all the way down the hall to her bedroom.

"Honey, Ben probably doesn't know any bedtime stories. How about I read you *Cinderella* again?"

"No. I want a new story."

"Let's get you into your pj's first and brush your teeth." Ellie gently guided her into the bathroom.

"Don't go, Ben!" Amy ordered before closing the bathroom door.

He waited in her girly bedroom, feeling like a bull in a china shop. The pink comforter had ruffles on the edges. A well-worn stuffed animal had a place of honor near the pillow while a small folded blanket rested at the foot of the bed. It had kittens on it. His gaze moved to the bedside table where a pile of picture books sat.

"Why can't Ben tell me a story?" Amy demanded as

she walked into the room with her mother and hopped into bed.

"Because he doesn't have children, so he doesn't know stories."

"I know stories," Ben said. Granted, none came to mind that he could relate to a five-year-old kid. But he was a Marine, which meant he was resourceful. Ben stared at the cover of the storybook on top of the pile next to Amy's bed. "I can do that. No problem. Once upon a time . . ." All fairy tales began that way, right? "Once upon a time, many years ago in the land of Wonder an evil lord ruled the kingdom. He'd been a good guy once, but then turned to the dark side. His name was . . . Sir Badlord. And he was feared by all the people in the land."

"Was he mean?" Amy asked.

Ben nodded solemnly. "Very mean."

"Hold on a sec, honey," Ellie said. "I need to speak to Ben."

"But he's telling me a story now," Amy protested.

"Yeah, I know. This won't take long."

Ellie tugged Ben off the bed to a corner of the room and leaned close to whisper, "The point of a bedtime story is not to give my daughter nightmares. Kids her age take things literally."

"Understood. It's not my intention to scare her. Trust me, okay?" He returned to Amy's bedside with Ellie close by his side.

"So what about Sir Badlord?" Amy asked. "What did he do? Blow up the world? Joshua in the reading group at the library is always blowing up the world and

32

making explosion noises. Does Sir Badlord do that?"

"Sometimes. But tonight, he and his gang of dark knights rode out into the night and captured Lady Blush, the daughter of . . . Guy of Nice. Now, Sir Guy was a nice guy."

"Was he a good daddy?"

"Yes."

"Did he love Lady Blush?"

"Absolutely."

"Mommy says my daddy loves me, but I don't think he's a very good daddy."

Ben wasn't sure how to respond to the little girl's confession. "I'm sorry to hear that."

"Me, too." She moved closer. "Tell me more."

"Well, like I said, Sir Guy was good and people liked him. He did good stuff."

"Like what?"

"Uh . . . good deeds. He officiated at jousts, spoke at . . . baptisms and generally speaking, he ate more chicken than he probably should have, but people liked Sir Guy. A lot better than they liked Sir Badlord. Which made Sir Badlord mad. So he came to Nice castle and took Lady Blush."

"Was she a princess?"

"Close enough. Anyway, this Sir Guy was beside himself. He knew he had to call on the only one who could get her back—one of the few, the proud. Sir Good-knight." Ben was really getting into it now. "Goodknight led his squad of knights, squires and pages—known as the Knights of the Black Stone—on many quests in the past. Like the Marines, he valued honor, courage and commitment. So Goodknight agreed to help Sir Guy to rescue Lady Blush. He and the rest of his team gathered to plan the mission and do some recon."

Ben didn't realize that he'd gone into a bit too much detail about reconnaissance and intelligence reports until he felt Ellie's hand on his arm. "She's fallen asleep."

"Some storyteller I am." Ben's voice was rueful. "It put the kid to sleep."

"It was quite creative for a Marine."

"Marines can be creative when the situation warrants."

"So Sir Guy ate more chicken than he should have, huh?"

Ben shrugged and stood aside while Ellie clicked off the light and checked the night-light before exiting the room, leaving Amy's door slightly ajar.

"Where did you come up with names like that?" she asked him.

He smiled ruefully. "My brothers accuse me of being too much of a punster."

"And do they accuse you of eating more chicken than you should?"

"Not if they're smart."

The transformation of his smile into a full-blown grin, complete with the hint of a dimple that would have done Dennis Quaid proud, drew her attention to his lips. She'd never momentarily lost her train of thought just by gazing at a guy's mouth before. "I . . . uh . . . I wanted to thank you for this evening." She had

34

to look away to regain her equilibrium. "The dinner was delicious."

"I'm glad you enjoyed it."

"And thanks for making up the story for Amy tonight. That was nice of you."

"I like to think that I can be a nice guy when needed."

"A regular knight in shining armor, huh? Like Sir Goodknight?"

One chestnut eyebrow lifted in a masculine challenge of her comment. "Anything wrong with that?"

"Nothing. As long as you realize that I'm no Lady Blush. I'm not a damsel in distress."

"You're saying you don't need a knight in shining armor to rescue you?"

"I could use the armor. Not the knight."

"You don't see yourself remarrying?"

"No."

"Why not? You're young and beautiful. Why can't you see a happy ending for yourself?"

"Marriage isn't a happy ending for me. Have you ever been married?"

"No."

"Well, trust me, it's not what it's cracked up to be."

"Amy said that she didn't think her dad was a good dad. Why is that?" Ben's expression darkened. "Did he hit her?"

"No, nothing like that."

The line of his jaw tightened. "Did he hit *you*?"

"No." Perry had never resorted to physical abuse. He hadn't had to when a sarcastic comment could do plenty of damage. To this day she wasn't sure if his intention had been to hurt her on any of those occasions, or if he'd simply been so self-involved that he hadn't cared how she felt. She suspected it was the latter.

"Then what happened?"

"Why do you care?" Ellie countered.

"Because I cared about John and you're his sister."

"I already told you that I don't need anyone looking after me."

"Humor me, okay? What can it hurt, telling me about your marriage? Unless you're still so in love with the guy that you don't want to talk about it."

"I don't want to talk about it, but not because I'm still in love with Perry. Oh, I loved him in the beginning. Blindly so. I met him in my freshman English class in college. He asked to borrow my notes and never gave them back. That should have been a clue that Perry was only out for Perry. But he was a sweet-talking charmer. Incredibly good-looking. He swept me off my feet, promised me the world. We got married a few months later and I quit school to support him. Dumb I know, but Perry made it seem like the most responsible plan. He could focus on getting his business degree and then he'd get a great job and I could stay home with the family we wanted. At least I thought we both wanted a family. Perry said he did. He said all the right things. And we were happy in the beginning. Then I got pregnant. That wasn't part of Perry's plan. Not until he graduated from college. Even so, he pretended to make the best of things. And I worked until a week before Amy was born."

"What happened then?"

"Perry acted like he was so proud of his baby daughter. He showed off pictures of her to everyone he met. But there were signs that things weren't going well. We were always short of money. Perry would come up with one get-rich scheme after another. This time, babe, he'd tell me. This time it's the real thing. But it never was. He graduated from college when Amy was two. A few weeks later we discovered that Amy has asthma."

Ellie sighed and sat on the couch, kicking off her sandals to curl her feet beneath her. Talking about her marriage made her feel sad and stupid. "Perry didn't take the news well. He likes perfection and suddenly Amy wasn't his perfect little girl any longer. He took off a few months later and we haven't heard much from him since."

Ben sat on the couch beside her. "He doesn't stay in contact with his daughter?"

"No. Not really. I keep telling her that her daddy loves her, and he probably does in his own shallow way. But Perry isn't really capable of loving anyone other than himself."

"Is he at least paying child support?"

He could feel Ellie retreating from him even though she didn't move. "Look, I shouldn't have gone on about things the way I did. I never meant to. When I'm tired, my mouth gets away from me sometimes." She leaned forward. "Can I get you something to drink? A can of soda maybe?"

"Relax." His hand on her arm prevented her from

leaping up and retreating to the kitchen the way she clearly wanted. "I'm fine."

Ben suspected that her refusal to answer his question about child support meant that slimebag Perry wasn't paying. No surprise there. The guy didn't sound like the responsible kind. He wouldn't make a good Marine.

John had never gone into any detail about his sister's ex-husband, other than referring to him as a dirtbag and much worse. Ben hadn't pushed him for more information, that wasn't his way. He wasn't sure now that John had known the exact specifics. Ben suspected Ellie had shielded her brother from the worst of what had really occurred in her marriage.

Ben's anger at her jerk of an ex-husband made him lose his focus on diplomacy. "You need money. I've got money." He reached for his wallet. "More than I need or could possibly use. Here." He held out a bunch of hundred dollar bills. "Take it."

"I'm *not* for sale. Not in this lifetime," Ellie growled, before leaping to her feet and pointing to the door. "Get out!"

Chapter Three

Ben realized his error immediately and jammed his wallet to his back jean pocket. "I'm sorry, I shouldn't have put it that bluntly."

"You shouldn't have said it at all." Ellie's voice vibrated with anger.

"Let me explain. Please. Hear me out."

Her look warned him that he'd better talk fast so he

did. "A little over a year ago I inherited a lot of money from my wealthy oil baron grandfather. I thought he'd disinherited me years earlier. He never really forgave my mom for marrying an unknown Marine from Chicago named Kozlowski. And he never approved of my brothers and me joining the Marine Corps instead of his oil company down in San Antonio. Anyway, I've got all this money that I did nothing to earn."

"Then give it to a charity."

"I'd rather give it to you.

"And I didn't mean to imply that you had to *do* anything to earn it," Ben quickly clarified before her mind went down that path. "I'm just trying to help out here."

"Don't. I'm not your responsibility. So thanks, but no thanks. I'm not accepting money from a stranger."

"If you get to know me better than I won't be a stranger."

"It won't change my mind."

"We'll see."

"You're incredibly stubborn." Her voice reflected her exasperation.

"So are you."

"Exactly. So don't go wasting your time thinking you can change my mind."

"Spending time with you is not a waste."

"It is if you think you can change my mind."

"Let me be the judge of that."

"You haven't talked much about Johnny," she noted, changing the subject abruptly. "Is that because you think that talking about him will upset me?"

It upset *Ben.* Not that he mattered in this equation.

Keeping his promise to his buddy by looking after Ellie was the only priority here. Nothing else was relevant. Not the fact that he was attracted to Ellie, that she made his heart beat faster, that the flash of her smile made him want to kiss her. All those things were totally irrelevant.

Telling himself that didn't make the feelings disappear. Reminding himself to stay focused, he belatedly answered her question. "I didn't want to say anything to upset you more than I have."

"My brother loved being a Marine. He loved being part of a team that way. I know Marines are a tight-knit group and Johnny had never been part of something like that before. I just wanted you to know that. I can't talk about it much right now. The wound is still too fresh."

Ben nodded. He understood better than she could possibly imagine. "Wound" was an accurate description.

In the Marine Corps he'd been trained that pain was weakness escaping the body. But what about guilt? That showed no signs of leaving him. Instead it haunted him, darkly gnawing away at his insides.

"I understand that it's too soon," he said quietly, "but we've got time. I'm not going anywhere. Like I told you earlier, I'm based near here at Camp Lejeune. I really want to get to know you and Amy better. With that in mind, how about we get together tomorrow?"

Ellie shook her head. "I don't think that's a good idea."

"What are you afraid of?"

"I'm not afraid of anything."

"We're all afraid of something."

"Even a big bad Marine like you?"

"Absolutely."

"Fine. Then what are you afraid of?"

"Snails," he said promptly. "They give me the creeps."

"Snails?"

"Hey, they're all slimy and stuff."

"They live in a shell."

"Yeah, well, maybe I should have said naked snails then."

"You're afraid of naked snails?"

"Affirmative."

"You're kidding me, right?"

"No. So what are you afraid of?"

"Not naked snails, I can tell you that much."

"Go ahead, make fun of a guy after he's bared his heart to you."

"You didn't bare your heart, just your phobias."

"Hey, I didn't say it was a phobia," Ben protested. "Just that I'm not fond of naked snails."

"Oh, so now you're backpedaling, are you? I believe the actual comment was that snails give you the creeps."

"They do. That doesn't mean I have a phobia about them. A phobia would be the fear of running across naked snails everywhere I go. Usually the subject doesn't come up that often. Unless I'm at a French restaurant. Getting back to you, you never said what you're afraid of. Come on." His sensual mouth quirked with an intimately teasing expression that made her heart skip. "There must be something?"

There were plenty of things. Of being a single mom responsible for a five-year-old daughter. Of what would happen to Amy if anything should happen to Ellie. Perry would be useless and his mom not much better. The thought of her daughter having to go into the foster care program the way Ellie and her brother had gave Ellie nightmares more nights than she cared to admit.

Because she knew from personal experience how quickly lives could change. Their dad walked out shortly before Johnny had been born and died shortly thereafter in a fire. They'd been raised by a single mom. When Ellie was seven her mother died in a car crash, killed by a drunk driver who crossed into her lane of traffic. The head-on collision killed her mom instantly.

There were no relatives to take them in so they'd gone into the system. The only good thing had been that, thanks to a compassionate caseworker, she and her brother had been allowed to stay together.

That was one of the reasons why the failure of her marriage had hit Ellie so hard. Because she'd desperately wanted to have a family, to have some security. To have someone to share the good times and the bad times with.

A tiny voice in her head wondered if having Ben in her life might not be a good thing. Marines had a reputation for being responsible. Maybe he would be dependable. Maybe he would be there for Amy should anything happen to Ellie. *Yeah, right.* She'd only known the guy a few hours and already she was turning him into a knight in shining armor despite her protests that she didn't need rescuing.

"Forget what you're afraid of," Ben said. "Tell me what makes you happy?"

"That's easy. My daughter."

"What else?"

"Chocolate. Dark chocolate." The rebellious thought crossed her mind that a sexy Marine like Ben might make her happy, but she quickly wiped it from her memory bank. She didn't believe in the happy endings found in her daughter's fairy tale books. Ellie knew from bitter experience that they rarely existed in the real world.

"Come on, girlfriend, give me all the details." Latesha made the demand as she and Ellie sat at a table, refilling paper napkins in the metal dispensers that went on every table. Al's Place was temporarily empty. A fellow waitress and friend, Latesha was slightly older than Ellie and a whole lot more outrageous. "I want every single itty-bitty juicy detail."

"There aren't any."

"Puhlease." Latesha rolled her brown eyes in disbelief. "You take off last night with Mr. Too Yummy For Words hot on your trail. So come on . . ." She scooted her chair closer. "Tell me what happened."

"Nothing happened. He took Amy and me out to dinner last night."

"And . . . ?"

"And he took us home again."

"And then . . . ?"

"And then he told Amy a really clever bedtime story." The first thing Amy had asked Ellie this morning was where Ben was and when he was going to tell her more about Sir Goodknight and Lady Blush.

"What about you? What kind of bedtime story did he tell you?" Latesha's grin was wicked.

Before Ellie could answer, Cyn joined them. In her mid-twenties, Cyn had a fondness for anything black or purple. She also loved silver jewelry with a Celtic design. With her blond hair and green eyes, she looked nothing like Latesha, but the two shared the same personality type. Cyn perched on the edge of the table. "What are you two talking about?"

"Ellie was just going to give me the juicy details about her night with Mr. Too Yummy For Words."

Ellie frowned. "His name is Ben and he didn't spend the night."

"I hate it when they take off after getting what they want," Cyn noted.

"It wasn't like that," Ellie vehemently denied.

"Then tell us what it was like," Latesha said.

"I'm trying to, but you keep interrupting me."

"I wasn't interrupting you, that was Cyn."

"It was not. You're the one who keeps talking."

Ellie cleared her throat. "Hello? Earth to girlfriends. Listen carefully."

"Yeah, Cyn, listen carefully."

"She was talking to you, Latesha."

Ellie sighed in exasperation. "I'm talking to both of you. Or trying to. Ben and I did not sleep together."

"Define sleep together," Latesha said.

44

"I mean we didn't . . . you know." Ellie waved her hand.

"Why not?" Cyn demanded.

"Because I just met him and because I'm a mother with a young daughter."

Latesha reached for another pile of paper napkins. "That doesn't mean you can't be attracted to a sexy bad boy like Ben."

"If you don't want him, can I have him?" Cyn asked.

"Forget it," Latesha said. "I have dibs on him. I talked about him first."

"Look at her face." Cyn pointed at Ellie. "She wants him for herself."

Ellie felt herself blushing. "I do not!"

"Puhlease." Latesha shook her head. "You should have seen your expression."

"You're imagining things," Ellie retorted.

"I'd like to imagine a few things about that hotshot." Cyn's smile was dreamy.

"He's a Marine." Ellie wasn't sure why she told them that. Maybe it was with the hope that they'd show some respect. She should have known better.

"Whooohoo!" Cyn just about smacked her lips. "I do enjoy a man in uniform."

"Yeah, and you enjoy them even better out of uniform," Latesha retorted. "We heard that when you were dating that cop."

"Well, it's true. What else do you know about this Ben? He's not married is he?"

Ellie shook her head. "I don't think so."

"What?" Latesha's eyebrows rose. "That's the first

thing you check out, girlfriend."

"He wasn't wearing a wedding ring." Ellie tried not to sound too defensive but she wasn't sure how successful she was.

Cyn waved her words away. "That doesn't always mean anything. Guys have been known to take off their wedding ring when they enter a place like this."

"Ben wouldn't do that." Ellie's voice was firm.

Cyn immediately picked up on that. "Oh, so you already know that much about him, huh?"

"He was a friend of my brother's."

Cyn's expression turned from teasing to compassionate. "Did he come to offer his condolences?"

"He came to offer me money."

"What?" Latesha and Cyn exclaimed in unison.

Ellie hadn't meant to say that, it had just slipped out. "Never mind . . ." Ellie grabbed several napkin dispensers and tried to make a quick getaway.

Latesha tugged her right back into her chair. "Forget it, girlfriend. You're not leaving until you tell us what you meant by that."

Ellie was saved, if you could call it that, by the appearance of their boss. JayJay Lange was the proverbial school yard bully all grown up. Cyn had described him as a cross between a rabid raccoon and a devious weasel. He did have sunken eyes, a thin frame, and a skinny dark mustache. He also had a mean streak a mile wide.

"I'm not paying you girls to sit around and gossip," JayJay growled from the door that led to his office in the back. "Cyn, you're not even scheduled to work

46

today. What are you doing here?"

She bounced off the table. "I came to pick up my check."

"Well, then get in here and sign for it," JayJay ordered. "You other two, get back to work."

"Yes, master," Latesha muttered under her breath.

"What did you say?"

"I said, yes, Mr. Lange." Latesha picked up the tray filled with the napkin dispensers that she'd refilled. "Later," she murmured to Ellie, the look in her eyes making it clear that she intended to follow up on this.

Ben walked into Al's Place a little before six that night to find the place fairly crowded already. He had no trouble finding Ellie. She was standing at the bar, waiting for Earl to fill a drink order. Her short denim skirt hugged her bottom and showed off her long legs. She was wearing a black tank top. She had her hair in the braid she'd worn last night when he'd taken her out to dinner.

He remembered brushing his fingers across the velvety soft skin on her nape when he'd helped her into her jean jacket.

She turned from the bar and almost rammed into him.

"Steady." His hands had automatically gone to her shoulders to steady her, but stayed after she regained her balance. Touching her set off internal land mines, making him want to tug her into his arms and kiss her.

"Sorry about that." She expertly maneuvered the tray filled with drinks against him and gained her freedom.

Watching her walk away he was struck again by the

graceful way she moved. The sway of her hips wasn't deliberately sexy but it made his blood hot anyway.

"Enjoying the view?" Earl the bartender asked him.

Instead of answering, Ben took a seat at the bar and helped himself to a few salty peanuts before ordering a beer.

"I checked you out with a few of my devil dog buddies who are still in the Corps." Earl placed a coaster in front of him and then set the mug of beer on it. "They tell me you're on the up and up. A good guy. I sincerely hope that's right."

"Why's that?"

"Because as a former jarhead I'd hate to have to fight a fellow Marine, but I will if you mess with Ellie. I wouldn't take kindly to the possibility of you upsetting her again as you did last night."

"Her brother was a close friend of mine."

"I know that. I know you were there when he was killed by friendly fire. Died in your arms, so I hear."

"You heard right." Ben's voice was bleak.

"I'm trusting that you're not here to seduce her while she's still grieving for her lost brother."

Ben's eyes narrowed dangerously. "And I'm trusting that you're mistaken in saying that to me."

Earl backed up, but not much. "I may be. I want your word, as a Marine, that you aren't here to hurt Ellie."

"You have my word. I'm here to help her, but she's too stubborn to let me do that."

"She's not the only one. Her friend Latesha is even more stubborn than Ellie." Earl nodded at the tall woman serving drinks nearby.

Ben fell quiet as he watched Ellie quickly disperse her order and return to the bar where he waited.

"What are you doing here?" she demanded.

"What, no hello?" he teased her. "No, glad to see you?"

"What are you doing here?" she repeated.

"I came to see if you and Amy would like to do pizza and a video tomorrow."

She placed another set of drink orders with Earl before answering Ben. "I'm working until midnight tomorrow."

"How about Sunday? Are you working then?"

"She's off Sunday," Earl answered on her behalf.

"Outstanding. Then how about pizza and a video Sunday night?"

Ellie watched him suspiciously. "Why?"

"Why?"

"I'm not going to change my mind. I already told you that."

"I know you did. It's just pizza and a video. Like I said, I'd like to get to know you better."

Ellie saw the evil eye that JayJay was sending her way. "Okay. I'll see you Sunday. You'd better leave now."

"Why? I'm a paying customer." He lifted the beer that Earl had served him.

Ellie took the tray refilled with new drinks. Then she warned Ben, "If you stay you have to promise me you won't make any trouble."

"I promise." He crossed his heart with his fingers, drawing her attention to his navy blue T-shirt and how well it fit. The wicked gleam in his light hazel eyes made her heart beat faster. But she refused to give in.

"I mean it. I can't afford to lose this job."

Ellie walked away before Ben could remind her that she could afford to lose this no-good job, if she'd only stop being so stubborn and accept his offer. But she was stubborn. She probably needed to be to survive what she had.

He hated to think of her or her little girl doing without when that was so easily changed. The money meant nothing to him. But it could make a world of difference to her and to Amy. He just had to convince her of that fact. But first he had to get to know her better before he could figure out the best way to get her to see reason.

So here he was, nursing a beer while he watched Al's Place fill up with a few women and a lot of men. The pool tables located at the back were soon obscured by the crowd and the smoke. He eventually moved from the bar to a tiny table, where he was served another beer by Latesha.

"You gonna sit there all night?" Latesha demanded an hour later.

"Probably." He gave her three twenties as a tip. "Unless you have a problem with that?"

"Not me. But my boss JayJay Mean-as-a-Snake Lange over there isn't too pleased." She tilted her head toward a skinny guy near a door marked Office. "He heard about you making trouble last night."

"All I did was stop some rowdy from pawing Ellie."

"That rowdy was one of JayJay's best friends."

"I don't care if he was the president's best friend,

that's no excuse for manhandling a woman."

"So you knew Ellie's brother?"

He nodded.

"She told me that you offered her money." Latesha narrowed her brown eyes at him. "Ellie isn't that kind of girl. So maybe it would be best if you took your cute self out of here and didn't do anything to make Ellie's life any more difficult than it already is."

"I'm not trying to make her life more difficult, I'm trying to make it easier."

"By offering her money?"

"That's right."

Latesha rolled her eyes. "And what do you want from her in return?"

"Nothing."

"Yeah, right."

"I'm serious. I promised Ellie's brother that I'd look out for her. I have some extra money that I don't need, and I want her to have it. Why is that so hard to believe?"

"People don't give money to strangers without there being a hitch. Without strings attached."

"No strings. I just want to help Ellie. Can you help me do that?"

Latesha eyed him suspiciously. "What do you mean?"

"I mean that you're a friend of hers, right?"

Latesha nodded. "So?"

"So maybe you could help me figure out how to convince her that she should accept my offer."

"Don't try and charm her, because that won't work. Her ex-husband was a smooth-talking charmer."

"Did you know him?"

Latesha shook her head. "I've just heard about him. Believe me, if I'd met him, I would have kicked his . . . butt. Walking out on his daughter that way." She shook her head. "Amy is such a little sweetheart. She deserves better."

"I totally agree."

"Then you'd better be good at proving that you really are better and not just another smooth-talking charmer. How about a burger to go with that beer?"

"Make it a cheeseburger with extra fries and you've got a deal."

"Just one more thing. I don't care if you are a Marine. You hurt Ellie or that little girl of hers and you'll have me to deal with. And Earl over there." She nodded toward the bartender, who was watching their inter-change with interest. "Earl will not take kindly to anyone upsetting Ellie. Understood?"

Ben nodded. "Understood. Loud and clear. Earl already warned me, by the way."

"He did?" Ben nodded, noticing the way that Latesha was staring at the burly bartender with unabashed interest. "Thanks for telling me that."

"No problem. Thank you for being such a loyal friend to Ellie. I'm glad that she has such loyal friends to help protect her."

As she walked away he could have sworn he heard Latesha mutter, "If this keeps up, we're gonna have to rename you Mr. Too Good To Be True."

"You look like a guy who could use some help." A

woman dressed in black pants and a purple shirt told Ben as he stared at the rows of movies in Vinnie's Video.

"It's that obvious, huh?"

"It is to me."

"I don't have any kids so I'm not sure what videos are good for a five-year-old."

"You don't have any kids," she immediately repeated. "Does that mean you're not married?"

He was startled by her question. "That's right."

"Good. I'm glad to hear that."

He eyed her warily. "Uh, I'm just looking for a video that a five-year-old girl would like."

"Amy, you mean. I work with Ellie over at Al's Place. My name is Cyn. And you're Ben, right?"

He nodded.

"Latesha told me you talked to her. Here, Amy hasn't seen this one yet." She pulled a video off the shelf. "It just came out two days ago. I hear you've already been warned not to hurt Ellie, right?"

"Right."

"So it might be redundant for me to repeat that warning, but hey, I'm gonna do it anyway."

"Is there anyone else in this town who's going to threaten to do me bodily harm if I hurt Ellie?" Ben demanded in exasperation.

"I could probably round up a few," Cyn cheerfully replied. "You've already met Frenchie, Ellie's next door neighbor and Amy's baby-sitter right? Trust me, you really don't want to get on her bad side. She's half-Cuban, you know. Or maybe her husband was Cuban.

Anyway, she lived in Paris, France, for a while. What I'm saying here is that Frenchie has international experience on derriere kicking, if you follow my drift. She's not your typical grandmotherly type, as you may have noticed."

"What makes you think I'm going to hurt Ellie? Or that she needs protecting from me?"

"I believe an ounce of prevention is worth a pound of cure, don't you?"

"I just want to help Ellie." He was getting tired of having to repeat that fact to everyone.

"And that's a good thing." Cyn patted him on the arm. "Nothing worth having comes easily, remember that. Here, Ellie hasn't seen this video." She handed him the latest release starring Sandra Bullock. "It's a chick flick, but you'll just have to grit your teeth and manage."

"I'm a Marine. I can handle a chick flick."

Cyn just smiled. "We'll see about that."

Ben fully expected the guy at Uncle Pete's Pizza to also warn him against hurting Ellie, but the older man just gave him the total for his bill and then handed him his order. The short drive to Ellie's ensured that the pizza was still warm when he arrived. He was greeted at the door by Amy.

"He's here, he's here!" The little girl was just about jumping up and down with glee.

"You must be really hungry," Ben noted with a grin. It was rewarding to have someone finally be glad to see him for a change. "Do you like pizza?"

Amy nodded then took him by his free hand and

tugged him inside. "Tell me more about Lady Blush."

"She likes pizza. And she's almost as pretty as your mom."

"I hope you remember where your story left off," Ellie said. "Because I'll warn you Amy has a very good memory."

Ben wondered if Ellie had a good memory too. He knew he did. That must be why he vividly recalled every instance that he'd touched her. She looked incredibly sexy in jeans and a pink T-shirt. Not fancy clothing, but Ellie didn't need to be fancy to get him all hot and bothered.

"Ben!" He was distracted by Amy, who'd just seen the picture on the video. "Is that our video?"

He nodded.

She grinned from ear to ear.

The kid was so easy to please. He just wished he could do more. Wishing is not a course of action for a Marine. He would make sure that he *did* do more.

Unfortunately he hadn't decided how ninety minutes later when the video was over and Ellie announced it was Amy's bedtime. Amy returned a few minutes later, wearing blue pajamas with grinning cats on them.

"Okay, tell me my story now, Ben." The little girl grabbed him by the hand and tugged him down the hall to her room.

"Did you brush your teeth?" Ellie asked her daughter as she got into bed.

"Does Lady Blush brush her teeth?" Amy asked Ben. He nodded. "All the time."

Amy shoved back the bedcovers and got out of bed.

"Hey, where are you going?"

"To get my toothbrush so I can brush my teeth all the time."

The look Ellie shot him said *See? I warned you. Kids take things literally.*

"I didn't mean she brushes her teeth all the time."

Amy frowned. "That's what you said."

"I know. That was a mistake. What I meant is that she brushes her teeth two or three times a day."

"Okay then." Amy jumped back in bed. "Start the story now, please."

"Once upon a time in the land of Wonder . . ."

"You left out many years ago," Amy reminded him.

"Oh right. Once upon a time, many years ago, in the land of Wonder an evil lord ruled the kingdom. When we last saw Sir Badlord he'd just snatched Lady Blush from her father Sir Guy at Nice Castle. Sir Goodknight has deployed on the mission to save her. Now, Badlord's castle was on a high hill with good sight lines to any possible attackers. He and his men decided on a night assault. They approached from the rear while planning a diversionary action at the front of the castle."

"What's divinary mean?" Amy stumbled over the unfamiliar word.

"Diversionary is something that's supposed to confuse the enemy, to make Sir Badlord look out the front of his castle and not out the back. Anyway, the plan was for Sir Rock to start playing music. Sir Rock was the minstrel of the Knights of the Black Stone and he had the only electric lute in the realm. He'd crank it up, go

56

to full distortion and lash out with a mean rendition of Queen's classic "We Are the Champions," a real crowd pleaser."

Amy stared at Ellie. "Mommy, why are you laughing?"

"Because I think Sir Rock is funny."

"How come?"

"He just is."

Ben continued. "While Sir Rock was belting out his music, the plan was for Sir Goodknight, or GK as he was known to his buddies, and the rest of his rescue team to scale the rear wall of Badlord's castle, surprise Badlord's men and rescue Lady Blush. Just past midnight, they assembled to start their mission. The wall team, led by Sir . . . uh . . . Sir Vine, was ready with grappling gear, ropes and ladders."

"Mommy, you're laughing again."

"Sorry." Ellie tried to look repentant.

"Sir Rock and his band were ready to rock and roll. GK put on his knight or K.N.I.G.H.T-vision goggles, the ones that let him see bad guys in the dark. Then he gave the signal for the mission to begin. Everything was going exactly according to plan. They got inside while all the guards were rocking to the music. GK hurried down to the dungeon. He unlocked the heavy door, opened it, only to find that the room was empty. Lady Blush was gone!"

Amy's big brown eyes got even bigger. "Where'd she go?"

"GK didn't know. He had to gather new intelligence."

"Maybe Lady Blush went home."

"I doubt it. But I'll tell you more about their adventures next time."

"I want to know *now*."

"It's past lights-out time," Ellie said.

"Will Lady Blush be okay?" Amy asked.

"I'm sure she will be. Right, Ben?" Her look warned him that she'd better be right or his head would be on a platter.

Ben nodded. "Right. Absolutely."

"What if she's not?" Amy said. "What if her daddy Sir Guy just leaves her lost? What if he doesn't work to find her?"

"He will and so will Sir Goodknight." Ben's voice was firm.

"What if her daddy thinks she's a bad girl and doesn't want her anymore?"

Ellie's heart ached at the thought that Amy was talking about herself and her own absent father. She took her daughter in her arms and hugged her reassuringly. "That would never happen. Because Lady Blush is almost as good a girl as you are, sweetie. And you know how many people love you tons. I do, and so does Frenchie and Cyn and Latesha."

"And daddy?"

"Your daddy loves you, too. He's just not good at remembering to say so. But he gave you Raboo to remind you." She handed Amy the well-worn stuffed yellow rabbit. It was one of the very few gifts Perry had given his daughter, a remnant from the first two years of her life when he'd acted the proud papa when it suited him to do so.

"Raboo is 'lellow," Amy sleepily informed Ben. "You can kiss him good night." She held the toy out to Ben.

As Ellie watched Ben awkwardly kiss Raboo, a little piece of her heart was lost. She tucked the covers around Amy and handed her the kitten blanket she nuzzled every night. "Now go to sleep."

"See you later, alligator."

"In a while, crocodile." The silly good-night rhyme was one of the few things Ellie remembered about her mother so she'd included it in her daughter's nightly ritual.

Once she and Ben were in the living room, he tugged her down on the couch with him. His original plan had been to play the chick flick video that Cyn had suggested, but he could tell that Ellie was too distracted for that at the moment. "You've gone all tense. It was that comment Amy made about her dad, wasn't it?"

Ellie nodded.

"Come here." He turned her so that she was in front of him. "You need to relax." He gently rubbed her shoulders. The pink T-shirt she wore was soft beneath his hands. She'd gathered her hair into a ponytail that swished as she moved her head.

Ellie turned to face him without realizing how close she was to him. Only a heartbeat away.

Then, even that tiny distance disappeared as Ben lowered his mouth to hers and kissed her.

Chapter Four

Ellie's eyes closed, focusing all her attention on Ben's kiss. His approach wasn't that of a conquering hero or a marauding warrior. Instead he temptingly, rhythmically brushed his lips back and forth against her mouth, coaxing her lips to relax, to part, and finally to cling.

His fingers trailed along her cheek, curving to cup her chin and remaining there as he deepened the kiss. He tasted and tested each corner of her mouth and the lush softness in between. He made her feel as if she were the sole reason he lived and breathed.

Ellie was shaken by how right this felt, by how perfectly his lips conformed to hers. His hands on her shoulders communicated both strength and tenderness as he pulled her closer into his embrace. His touch inflamed her. He seemed to instinctively know how to bring her pleasure, when to slow down, when to move forward. Logical thought was overwhelmed by an avalanche of physical pleasure.

Ben undid her hairclip, freeing her hair to tumble over her shoulders. He tunneled his hand beneath the silken mass to brush his fingertips against her nape. His other hand slid beneath the hem of her T-shirt to cup the small of her back, feathering his thumb along her spine.

Things intensified rapidly from there, blossoming into a hungry exchange of darting tongues and sultry caresses. His husky murmurs of excitement spurred her on. Pressed tightly against him, she felt the hardening contours of his body.

Sensual hunger prowled through her body. They were erotically in sync in a way that she'd never experienced before. He inspired a response that she could neither understand nor control.

It wasn't until he lowered her to the couch and they were both horizontal that the reality of her position struck her. And as it did so, she panicked, rolling away, out from beneath his sexy body and all the temptation it had aroused. She quickly stood, needing to regain control, to be on her own two feet again.

Her mouth still throbbed from his sensual kisses and the desire to return to his embrace remained. But it was overpowered by the fear of what had almost occurred. She'd only known this man a few days. The unexpected intensity of her response floored her. She wasn't the type to go all weak at the knees over a hunky guy. Not since Perry.

Was this history repeating itself? Was she in danger of making a fool of herself over another good-looking charmer who'd say whatever she wanted to hear to get what he wanted?

She took several steps back as he sat up.

"You'd better go." Her voice sounded rusty.

"Ellie . . ."

Even the husky way he said her name was powerful, but she couldn't afford to be weak. She needed to keep her focus on her daughter. "This isn't going to work."

"What isn't?"

"This situation. I think it would be best if you didn't come by again."

"Do you really think that's what would be best for Amy?"

He scored a major hit on her Achilles' heel. Her daughter had clearly fallen for Ben. "Why are you doing this?"

"Kissing you?"

"All of it. Telling Amy bedtime stories. Bringing us pizza."

"I want to get to know you better and for you and Amy to get to know me."

"Why?"

He couldn't tell her the real reason, that guilt drove him, tortured him, kept him awake at night. "I've already told you why."

"Because you promised my brother you'd look out for us. And I've already told you that's not necessary."

"Look, let's just take things one day at a time, okay? Amy seems happy to see me, to listen to my stories."

He was right. Amy was more than happy; she was blossoming under his attention. She clearly loved spending time with him, and he was incredibly good with her. Ellie hated to upset her daughter, who had already had so many disappointments in her young life.

"All right. We'll take things one day at a time. But no more kissing."

"You didn't enjoy it?"

"That's irrelevant. The bottom line is that I'm not looking for any more complications in my life."

"Understood." Ben wasn't exactly hoping to mess up his life any further either. But the first touch of her lips against his had created enough voltage to light up the entire eastern seaboard. He'd never anticipated his growing attraction to his friend's sister. His *deceased* friend's sister.

Had John lived, he would have patted Ben on the shoulder, claimed he'd done the matchmaking himself, and then demanded to know Ben's intentions. And all the while he'd have had that slightly lopsided grin on his face.

But John wasn't alive. And a good part of that was Ben's fault. He should have done a much better job at protecting his friend.

It was too late for that now. But it wasn't too late to fulfill his friend's final dying wish. Whatever it took, Ben planned on looking after Ellie and her daughter.

"Ben's here, Ben's here!"

Ellie had heard her daughter shout those words a number of times over the following week. One rainy day he'd brought a picnic lunch they'd shared on the living room floor, another morning he'd shown up with hot cinnamon rolls and a kite to fly in the park.

She had to give him credit. He hadn't made any further moves on her. Not that he'd been entirely at fault for what had happened Sunday night. She'd responded to his kiss like a character out of *Sex and the City*. Not that she had cable, but Cyn did and had filled Ellie in on the show's details.

"Ben's here, Ben's here!" Amy repeated.

Ben couldn't help it, he got a kick out of Amy's excitement at seeing him. He could only wish that Ellie were equally pleased.

She hadn't referred to that unbelievable kiss they'd shared. He wondered if she ever thought about it. He sure did, as much as he tried not to.

Amy tugged on his hand, returning his attention to her. "Can we go to Pirate's Palace today? I'm dressed like Lady Blush. See?" Amy twirled around in her princess costume. "Please, please can we go to Pirate's Palace?"

"Sure." Ben wasn't sure what Pirate's Palace was, but it sounded like some kind of amusement park.

"Yeah!"

"Don't shout," Ellie said, joining them from the kitchen.

Ben thought she looked great in a pair of jeans and a white peasant top with some kind of red embroidery around the edges. He especially appreciated the amount of pale skin displayed by the top's neckline.

"We're going to Pirate's Palace!" Amy did a happy dance, the skirt of her pink dress billowing out around her. "Ben said so."

"He did?" Ellie eyed him warily.

Amy gazed up at him with those big brown eyes of hers. "Tell her, Ben. Tell her you said yes."

"Uh, what is Pirate's Palace?"

"The miniature golf place across from the supermarket."

"Miniature golf?" He repeated, trying not to sound as horrified as he felt.

Ellie nodded. "Do you have a problem with that?"

Of course he did. Real men didn't play miniature golf. But he'd already agreed to take Amy, so there was no way he was going back on his word. "No, no problem at all."

"So, Ben, have you played much miniature golf?" Ellie asked.

"Enough to get by." Which wasn't a lie. Even though he'd never stepped foot on a miniature golf course or whatever they were called, it couldn't be hard to figure out. He managed complex battle strategies so he was sure this would be no problem. "How about yourself?"

"Never."

Thank heaven. Then she wouldn't know if he was doing something wrong. Outstanding. This was working out just fine.

"Amy hasn't, either," she added.

Also outstanding. It wouldn't do to be shown up by a five-year-old.

"But she's been wanting to ever since she first saw the place and the castle they have."

"It's not as big as Sir Guy's, I bet. Are we going now?" Amy took each of their hands in hers and tugged impatiently.

"We sure are."

"I like this," Amy announced, beaming up at them.

"I like it, too," Ben said. And he meant it.

"Outstanding," Amy said, using one of his phrases and further stealing his heart in the process.

Ten minutes later Ben stared at the outlandishly tacky environs of the Pirate's Palace with an expression of disbelief. The place was built into a hillside and had dragons, a pirate's ship, windmills, fountains and lots of green indoor-outdoor carpeting tying all the visually clashing sections together.

"Does Sir Guy's castle look like that?" Amy pointed to the garishly painted, multi-turreted facade that was the centerpiece.

"I sure hope not," he muttered.

"What, black and purple aren't your colors?" Ellie teased him. "A friend of mine from work loves them."

"Cyn?" he guessed.

"How did you know her name?"

"I think I ran into her at the video store when I stopped there the other day. She told me she was a friend of yours."

"What else did she say?"

"Not much."

Ellie wasn't buying that for a second. "That doesn't sound like Cyn. She always has something to say. Usually something outrageous. What aren't you telling me?"

"That your swing needs some work." Ben stepped closer until he was right behind her. "Here, try holding the club like this."

He reached around her, bracketing her with his arms. He'd rolled up the sleeves on his light blue shirt to reveal his muscular forearms. She could feel his body heat radiating from his chest to her back. He cradled her hands in his, his fingers wrapped around hers.

The swivel of his hips as he practiced the swing further cupped her bottom against him. She was so distracted that when she finally stepped away to try it on her own she dropped the golf club entirely. Despite the fact that she was battling her Halloween princess costume that kept getting in her way, Amy was still doing better than Ellie was.

But then Ellie was coping with a major distraction supplied by one terribly sexy Marine named Ben. Even though he wasn't in uniform he still carried himself with a powerful self-assurance that was as much a part of him as his hazel eyes.

"Here, let's try that again." He stepped closer and once again she was encircled by temptation. "Remember aim, swing, release. Only don't let go of the club this time." He doubted any of that was proper golf terminology. But hey, Ben figured he was doing pretty well here, all things considered. And the chance to hold Ellie in his arms was an unexpected benefit.

The top of her head was just beneath his chin. He could smell the lemony shampoo she used on her soft hair. The sexy feel of her denim-clad bottom pressed against him was enough to drive him mad.

"I've got it now," she said. "You can let me go."

He did so reluctantly. He felt a surprising sense of loss without her in his arms.

"Watch me, watch me!" Amy squealed.

"Be careful," Ellie said. "Don't swing the club too much or you might hit someone. Just put it in front of the ball."

When they'd first started out, Amy thought the club was some new version of a baseball bat, like the one she'd seen kids playing with in the park across from their apartment building. Ben had been the one to convince her that the ball was supposed to stay on the ground and that she was supposed to tap it with the club.

Ellie was struck yet again by how incredibly good Ben was with Amy. She wondered if he had nieces and nephews that made him so good with kids. She'd been dying to ask him but hadn't wanted to seem too nosy.

"Great shot!" Ben congratulated Amy. "Give me a high five, Lady Amy. Way to go!"

Amy's grin was huge. "I did good."

"You sure did."

"Outstanding."

"Yeah, outstanding." He and Amy shared a grin as he reached down to ruffle the little girl's hair. "Now let's see if you can hit the ball into the dragon's mouth."

"Does Lady Blush have a dragon scarin' her?"

"I guess we'll have to see when I tell you more of the story tonight. Do you think she should have a dragon scaring her?"

"Only if her mommy or Sir Goodknight can save her right away. You never told me about Lady Blush's mommy. Where is she?"

Ben scrambled for an answer. "Uh, she's away on business."

"Oh. My mommy never goes away." Amy gazed up at him with solemn eyes. " 'Cept when she has to work and then I stay with Frenchie. But even when I gots to go to the hops-ital sometimes, my mommy always stays with me. Then I'm not so scared. Mommies are good at that."

"Good at what?"

"At making you feel better."

"Yeah, my mom makes me feel that way, too."

"You're too old to have a mommy."

"Ouch." He winced before laughing.

"If mommies are good at making you feel better, kids are good at putting you in your place," Ellie noted with a grin. "You don't have any kids of your own?"

"No. Never been married, never had kids. But I plan to."

"You're good with them," Ellie said. "Do you have a lot of nieces and nephews or something?"

"It must be 'or something,' because only one of my brothers is married. Striker. And he's only been married a year. No kids yet."

Finally, a time when the discussion of his personal life came naturally and didn't seem too invasive. "Do you come from a big family?"

"I have four brothers. All Marines."

"It must have been nice growing up in a big family. Johnny and I only had each other." She bit her lip as a wave of emotion hit her, as it often did at unexpected moments. She'd hear the phone ring and think it might be her brother; she'd check the mailbox and wonder if there might be a letter from him. And then she'd remember. There wouldn't be any more calls or letters from Johnny. He was gone.

It was still so hard for her to accept. Most of the time she just pretended he was still overseas, doing his thing, loving his life as a Marine.

Denial for sure. But sometimes it was the only way to make it through a day.

She'd done the same thing when their mom had died

in a car crash. She and Johnny had pretended that they were only temporarily staying in a foster home until their mom came back for them. In reality they knew that would never happen, but some days denial made reality easier to cope with.

Eventually the emotions caught up with you, though. She knew that. It usually happened at night, when Amy was asleep. Then the panic would hit, the realization that Ellie was alone in her responsibility for her daughter. Sure, Perry was out there someplace. And his mother played a small part in Amy's life. But basically Ellie was on her own.

That's when the loneliness would set in, and the regrets that her daughter didn't have the life Ellie had planned for her.

Ellie had wanted her daughter to grow up in a secure home with two parents who loved her and each other. So she'd stayed with Perry, and done things she'd regretted like leaving college, because she'd loved him and believed in the dream of their life together.

"Yeah, big families are especially interesting when there's only one bathroom," Ben was saying. "My dad had to set up a rotating schedule, and then a strict timetable. We learned very early to take showers the Marine Corps way."

"And what way is that?"

"Fast and efficient."

"I didn't think the Marine Corps actually had a special way of taking showers."

"Of course they do. All Marines learn it in boot camp."

"You're kidding me, right?"

He shook his head.

Amy tugged on his hand. "Ben, it's your turn to hit the ball into the dragon's mouth."

As she watched her daughter, Ellie reminded herself that falling for Ben would be like putting her head in a dragon's mouth. Not a safe thing to do at all.

"So what do you think?" Ellie asked her friends at work the next day. They were gathered around a table, refilling the red plastic ketchup squeeze containers with the thinned-down mixture JayJay used to save money. Al's Place wasn't officially open for another fifteen minutes. "Am I being an idiot?"

Cyn answered first. She eyed Ellie's tank top. "Well, personally I don't think that shade of pink goes with that lipstick color you're wearing."

"I'm not wearing any lipstick," Ellie denied.

Cyn squinted at her. "The boss man must have turned down the lights in here again."

"Or your eyes could be going," Latesha said.

Ellie waved her hands to regain their attention. "I wasn't talking about my appearance, I was talking about Ben."

"Are you being an idiot for being attracted to Mr. Too Yummy for Words hunky-Marine Ben?"

Ellie frowned. "I never said I was attracted to him."

"Who wouldn't be attracted to a fine specimen like him?"

"I meant am I being an idiot for letting Amy get more attached to him? She's so excited whenever he shows up that her face lights up. I haven't seen her this happy since before her father left. Maybe I should have done more to get him to keep up his visits, to stay in touch with her."

"How can you do that when you don't know where he is?"

"His mother must know, although she claims she doesn't. But I'm sure she sends him money whenever he needs it."

"If she has money to spare why doesn't she give it to Amy to help with her care?"

"Because Mrs. Jensen blames me for Perry leaving. In her book, her perfect son can do no wrong. But at least she does call Amy every now and then, and she does do her part to make Amy's birthday and Christmas nice."

"Big deal. The woman bad-mouths you every chance she gets. You think I haven't heard her? She came into Vinnie's Video to rent a video and I heard her telling some other woman how evil her ex-daughter-in-law is."

"What was she renting?" Latesha asked.

"The latest Vin Diesel film. It seems she likes that violent action stuff."

"Or she just likes buffed-up beefcakes like Vin," Latesha countered.

Cyn nodded. "You can never tell with these uptight blue-rinsed hair gals. They can surprise you."

Ellie had to laugh.

Latesha grinned. "There now, are you feeling better?"

"Oh, yeah," Ellie noted wryly. "It's really reassuring

to hear that my ex-mother-in-law is trash talking me behind my back."

"Would it make you feel better to know that I didn't let her check out the Diesel video because of outstanding overdue charges I invented on her account?" Cyn asked.

"Won't that get you into trouble?"

"Vinnie is my cousin. He dislikes your ex-mother-in-law as much as I do. She tells him his shelves are too dusty, which they aren't and I should know because I dust them every other day. And she says that he should use disinfectant on the plastic video cases. She cleans them with those little pop-up antiseptic wipes before taking them out of the store with her. I think she just likes complaining."

"Getting back to Amy, do you think I'm doing the right thing in allowing Ben to spend time with us?"

"You just said that you haven't seen Amy happier in years," Cyn pointed out.

Ellie nodded. "That's true."

"What about you?"

"Me?"

"Yeah, you. Ellie Jensen." Cyn pointed directly at her. "What about you? Are you happy to be spending time with Ben?"

Ellie could tell where this was going. "There's nothing going on between us. I told him that when he kissed—"

Cyn squealed. "He kissed you and you didn't tell us." She playfully smacked Ellie's arm. "You've been holding out on us, girlfriend! When did this happen?

When you were snuggled against him playing miniature golf yesterday?" At Ellie's startled look, she said,
"What? You think word about that wouldn't get back
to me? When another cousin of mine owns the
place?"

"Ben was merely showing me how to play . . ."

"Ohhh, yeah, I'm sure he was showing you how to
play." Ellie tossed a scrunched up napkin at her, but
Cyn expertly ducked out of the way. "So when and
where did this kiss take place?"

"Forget when and where," Latesha countered. "First
tell us how it was? Is he a good kisser?"

"Look at her face." Cyn pointed at Ellie. "It's written
all over it."

Ellie knew when she was beaten. Her two rowdy
friends weren't going to give her a moment's peace
until she answered their nosy question. "Okay, yes, Ben
is a very good kisser."

"I'm so glad you think so," he said from behind her.

Chapter Five

Ellie couldn't believe her bad luck. Of all the times for
Ben to stroll into Al's Place. She had no idea how to
extricate herself from this situation so instead of
defending herself, she went on the offensive. She added
a glare for good measure. "You should announce your
presence instead of sneaking around."

Ben didn't appear to be the least bit repentant. "Why
would I want to do that when this way I get to hear
something good?"

"Because it's the polite thing to do and Marines are supposed to be polite. Isn't that right, Earl?" The bartender had just joined them after hauling up a new order of alcohol from the storage room in the basement.

"Whatever it is, don't draw me into it," Earl calmly said.

"Semper fi." Ben looked mighty pleased with himself.

"The Marines are ganging up against us." Cyn folded her arms against her chest, a sure sign that she was getting aggravated.

"Earl, honey, how can you take Ben's side in this against mine?" Latesha stared at him, her lower lip stuck out in a grown-up version of a pout that Amy had perfected at the age of two.

"I wasn't doing that." Earl seemed real eager not to let Latesha think badly of him. He even came to her side as if his presence would reassure her of his sincerity.

"I'm so relieved to hear that," she purred.

Earl shot Ben a look as if to say sorry, you're on your own, buddy.

Latesha kissed him on his cheek as a reward.

"I'm not a kid to be given a peck and sent along," Earl growled abruptly. "The next time you kiss me, you'd better mean it." He stomped away.

Latesha rushed off in the opposite direction.

Ellie turned to Ben. "Now look what you've done."

He blinked. "Me?"

"Yes, you. If you hadn't walked in when you did, then Earl and Latesha wouldn't have fought."

"That was no fight," Ben scoffed. "It didn't even qualify as a skirmish."

"You. Outside." Ellie grabbed Ben's arm and yanked on it. "Right now. I want to talk to you."

"I'm guessing you're about to discover what a real fight is, Ben," Cyn called after him.

Ben let Ellie tug him outside. Not because he had to, but because he wanted to. He wanted to talk to her alone. She'd gone out of her way to avoid that the past few days.

He'd forgotten how incredibly sexy she looked when she was all riled up this way. She was wearing a pink tank top today along with her customary work attire of a short denim skirt. Her creamy skin was flushed, her gorgeous brown eyes held the fire of anger in them.

Passionate anger. But then Ellie was a passionate woman. He knew that from the way she'd kissed him.

And when he'd walked in and heard her telling her friends that he was not just a good kisser, but a *very* good kisser, he'd felt ten feet tall. She was trying to cut him back down to size now, but there was no going back from what she'd said.

Ellie put her hands on her hips and glared at him. "Are you proud of yourself?"

He wasn't sure how to answer that question so he said nothing. Besides, he'd rather look at her than talk. Well, actually, he'd rather kiss her than look at or talk to her. But he'd agreed not to do that again.

"You promised me that you weren't going to make any trouble." She paused as she realized that he was staring at her lips as if fascinated by them. "What's wrong? Is something wrong with my face?"

"Not a single thing." His voice had gone all husky. "Your face is perfect."

"Then why are you looking at me so strangely?"

"Define strangely."

Doing that would mean focusing on him and she was trying to avoid doing that. Because he looked entirely too good for her peace of mind. She should be used to his appearance by now. He was wearing jeans and a T-shirt she'd seen before. Nothing special. It's not as if he'd turned up in dress blues or something. He just looked good. Better than good. Awesome, really. She got a buzz just seeing him.

Don't go there, she warned herself. He's deliberately trying to provoke you. You survived Amy as a crabby two-year-old, a stubborn three-year-old, an inquisitive four-year-old. You can handle one sexy Marine.

That was the problem. She *oh, so much* wanted to handle this Marine. She wanted to run her hands up his chest, to feel his thundering heartbeat beneath her fingertips. She wanted to kiss him, wanted to experience the thrusting sensuality of his tongue mating with hers, of his body surging into hers.

Oh, my!

It had to be hormones. Out of whack, I-need-sex hormones. She'd just finished her period two days ago, maybe that's where these sudden X-rated thoughts were coming from.

That had to be it. Not because she had feelings for Ben. That wasn't an option.

"Define strangely," Ben repeated, moving a little closer. "Tell me how I was looking at you?"

He was deliberately pushing her buttons. Did he think she'd submissively back off? Or melt in his arms? Not her.

"Listen, buddy, this seduction routine is not going to work with me." She jabbed her finger at his chest for good measure, ignoring the jolt of awareness that brief contact created. "And you want to know why?"

"I'm dying to know why."

He said it as if he was dying to kiss her. She didn't even know how he managed to do that, convey that thought to her without saying it.

"Because I don't play games."

"You played miniature golf the other day. And I seem to recall you beating the pants off me the other night in a fierce game of Candy Land."

She got distracted for a moment or two by the visual image of Ben with his pants off.

"Don't be mad."

Darn it, he was using that voice, the one that would melt steel.

She tried to be strong, tried to hang on to anger even though it had already petered down to mere aggravation. "Then don't be impossible."

He quirked an eyebrow at her. "What makes me impossible?"

"I hardly know where to begin." If he thought he was charming his way out of this one, he was mistaken.

"Would it help if I said I was sorry?"

"Only if you really mean it."

"I've never had anyone doubt my sincerity as much as you do."

"I don't trust easily," she admitted.

"I realize that." He reached out to tuck a loose strand of hair behind her ear. "Which is why I'm working very hard to earn your trust."

Ellie leaned closer. He was no longer touching her but he was drawing her in with his presence, tempting her to make the first move, to give in to the emotions and desires racing through her body. It was as if an invisible cord tied them together, binding her heart to his.

Her gaze flew to his. She had no trouble reading his thoughts. He wanted her. The fire she saw smoldering in his light hazel eyes confirmed that fact. She was so close now that she could see how dark his eyelashes were. Why hadn't she noticed that before?

Her lips parted and her tongue darted out to lick her suddenly dry lips. Her heart stopped, her mind went blank. She was totally immersed in Ben—consumed by the spicy smell of the soap he used, by the feel of his breath on her skin. Mere inches separated them when the sound of a car backfiring nearby made her jump, interrupting the magical spell he'd woven around her.

"I . . . I . . . I have to get back to work." She turned to go back inside.

"Wait." His hand on her bare arm rekindled the fire within her. "I think we need to talk."

She shook her head. "Not here. Not now."

"Then when?"

"I work until midnight."

"Tomorrow then. Are you off during the day?"

"Yes, but I'll be busy all day."

"Doing what?"

It was none of his business but she didn't have the time to argue with him. "Cleaning the apartment."

He waved his hand as if dismissing her words. "I'll see you at your place."

He was gone before she could protest. Not that it would have done much good. Ben had the unmistakable air of a man who knew what he wanted and wasn't letting anyone stand in his way of getting it.

Ellie was vacuuming, moving the multi-filtered machine over the hardwood floors to the beat of a Madonna song being played on the portable radio, and almost didn't hear the sound of the doorbell.

She opened the door to find Ben standing there. He held out a bag filled with cleaning materials. "I've come to help you."

"Thanks for the offer, but . . ."

"That was not a yes or no question. It was a statement."

"So the Marine has spoken, is that it?"

"That's it."

She decided to call his bluff. "Okay, fine. Come on in. You can work in the kitchen." Surely a macho guy like him would have a problem accepting that assignment.

But no, he dug right in. And he was thorough, too, not just half-heartedly wiping a cloth over the counters and stove but cleaning behind the canisters and removing the liners from around the burners.

As she finished dusting the living room she was

aware of the heated looks Ben was sending her way. She was wearing an old pair of denim cutoffs and a faded blue T-shirt from Granny's Pancake House, hardly sexy attire, although the frayed cutoffs were a little on the short side. Especially when she'd bend over. She tried not to do that.

"Nice T-shirt," he noted.

She checked his expression to see if he was mocking her. But he appeared to be sincere. Or maybe he was just trying to make conversation. She couldn't fault him for that. "It's from my former place of employment."

"Must have been quite a jump going from Granny's Pancake House to a place like Al's."

"I've survived worse. Granny Baxter, she's the one who ran Granny's, she took it hard. Having to close her business after forty years. But times are hard and business was down, so she had to do what she had to do. She wasn't real pleased that the only place I could find a job was at Al's. She claimed that JayJay was a few pancakes short of a stack. It was one of her favorite insults. Anyway, she and her husband moved down to southern Georgia to retire. I got a postcard from them the other week." Ellie pointed to the front of her fridge, which was decorated with two of Amy's drawings.

"Where is Lady Amy?" Ben asked, before wiping the outside of the fridge, including the top which was always hard for her to reach.

"She's at a friend's house. It's best to have her out of the apartment while I'm cleaning so that she doesn't breathe in any of the dust I may be stirring up. It's bad for her asthma."

"It's my understanding that asthma can be managed."

"It can be if you have the right physician and other medical support people all working together and not against you. And if you find the right treatment program for each individual. Amy has an inhaler and she knows how to use it. I make sure that wherever she is, at Frenchie's next door or at a playmate's house, that they have information about her treatment as well as contact numbers for me and for Amy's doctor."

"I also read that there are certain triggers that can set off an asthma attack."

"That's right. Last year Amy was begging to have a kitten but with her condition the doctor said it isn't a good idea."

"Tell me what to look for so that I'll know if she's having an attack."

"Difficulty breathing, coughing, wheezing."

Ben nodded, the look on his face serious. "Yeah, that's what I read online but I just wanted to make sure that there wasn't something different I should look for in Amy's case."

"You read up on asthma?"

"Why do you sound so surprised?"

"It's just that Perry had no interest in the disease."

His expression darkened. "How many times do I have to tell you, I'm nothing like your sleazebag ex-husband?"

"He wasn't always a sleazebag." Otherwise how stupid was she to have married someone with absolutely no redeeming qualities. That had always been the problem. Perry had just enough charm to draw you in and make you hope.

"I can't believe you're defending him after the way he's treated you and Amy."

"He never mistreated me, never hit me or Amy. He can be very charming when he wants to be."

"When he wants something, you mean."

"There were times when he was very good with Amy, when she was a little baby. Maybe I should have done more to ensure that he'd be a better father." That's where Ellie's real guilt lay. Maybe if she'd been a better wife, if she'd been more tolerant, if she'd done more . . .

"Like what? What could you have done? Especially since he's apparently disappeared without letting you know where he is."

"I don't know." Ellie drifted into the kitchen to join Ben. "It's just that I see how much Amy hangs on your every word . . ."

"Yeah." He smiled. "That is pretty outstanding, isn't it."

"It makes me realize how much she's missed having a father, having that kind of male influence in her life. She had my brother but now he's gone too."

"John talked about you all the time, you know." Ben's voice was quiet. "He was always bragging about his smart sister and his cute niece."

"And I was always bragging about my brother the Marine. I still can't believe he's gone." Her voice was unsteady.

"I know." Ben cupped her cheek with his hand. "It's real tough."

She nodded and stepped away. Talking about her brother revealed more of her vulnerabilities than she wanted. Time to change the subject. She opened the fridge, welcoming the blast of cold air against her hot face. "Would you like something cold to drink?"

She didn't realize Ben was standing right behind her until he reached around her for a soda from the top shelf. Momentarily distracted by the warmth of his body pressed against hers, she didn't say anything until it was too late.

A spray of soda hit him in the chest the moment he pulled the tab top on the can. She barely jumped out of the way in time to avoid getting splattered herself.

"I usually prefer drinking my soda rather than bathing in it," he noted dryly. Setting down the still foaming can in the sink, he then peeled off his soaked T-shirt, yanking it over his head and then dropping it into the sink.

"I'm sorry about that." She dabbed at his bare chest with a paper towel, her fingers brushing against his muscular flesh. "I meant to warn you that Amy was playing with that soda can before putting it in the fridge. That's why I put it aside from the others. We went to the grocery store earlier today . . ."

"It's okay."

But it wasn't okay to be feeling what she was feeling when she touched him.

Yet she didn't seem to be able to step away. Not yet. Her hands remained poised on his warm skin, her fingers splayed. His heart beat beneath her open palm.

Her gaze lifted to his. Standing this close, she could

see the flecks of green in his light hazel eyes. She also saw the faint scar running along the right side of his jaw. "How did you get this?" She ran her fingertips along his skin, noting the seductive friction caused by the roughness of his morning's growth of beard, the shadowy stubble barely making an appearance on his face but adding a slightly dangerous element to his appearance.

"I fell when I was sixteen. Hit my jaw on the edge of a table and needed twenty stitches."

"You must have fallen pretty hard."

"A bad habit of mine," he murmured huskily, lifting a strand of her hair between his fingers and rubbing it as if enjoying the silky feel. "I don't fall often, but when I do, I fall hard."

He was a master of saying one thing and possibly meaning another. "So do you have any scars elsewhere?"

"Not that show."

Yeah, Ellie knew how that was. Knew that some scars were carried inside. They healed, but they never really disappeared. You worked around them.

Her gaze wandered to the bulldog tattoo on his upper arm. "Did that hurt when you had it done?"

He shook his head.

Her eyes returned to his face, to the intensity of his eyes, to the almost brooding way he was looking at her. "What's wrong?"

"Nothing." He stepped away from her. "I'm fine."

She had the feeling that he wasn't, but she had no idea how to get him to open up to her. There were times when she'd catch a glimmer of a painful darkness in his eyes at odds with his usually upbeat nature and she'd wonder . . . who or what had hurt him so much that he had to hide his pain so deeply? Did it have something to do with her brother or was it something or someone else?

She shouldn't care so much. She should leave well enough alone and keep her distance. That would be the wise thing to do.

It would also be wise to focus on the matter at hand. Him half-naked in her kitchen.

"Doing the laundry is next on the list, so you might as well add your T-shirt to the basket." She pointed to several very large baskets near the front door.

"What is Raboo doing in the laundry?" Ben asked, holding Amy's favorite stuffed animal up.

"Raboo gets washed every week."

"Which explains his rather well-worn look."

"Washing in very hot water kills dust mites, one of Amy's triggers. That's why I keep the apartment the way I do—clean and uncluttered. It's why I don't have toys just sitting out on the shelves in her room, why there aren't any pictures on the walls, why I use shades instead of blinds or drapes and why I have that expensive air filter always going in her room."

"Sounds like a lot of extra work."

"Amy is worth it." Ellie picked up one of the baskets.

"Of course she is." He picked up two of the others. "Where are we going with this stuff?"

"To the Laundromat down the street."

Ben insisted they go in his black Bronco. He took the

second basket from her and put it in the back seat before holding the passenger door open for her. He always made a point of doing things like that—helping her on with her jacket, holding the chair out for her at a restaurant, waiting until she sat down before sitting down himself. Taking care of her as he was now, by running up to her second-story apartment to get the remaining laundry basket.

To prevent herself from staring at him, she looked at her car, sitting forlornly in the neighboring parking space.

When Ben joined her, she said, "Tiny is starting to get the impression you don't like her." She opened the window. It was a beautiful spring day. The sun was shining and the wisteria was blooming along the chain link fence beside the parking lot.

Spring was pollen season, which meant that Ellie kept the apartment and car windows closed for Amy's sake. They'd been lucky that day they'd played miniature golf, because a front had moved in and the pollen levels were very low that week.

Ben backed up the Bronco. "And Tiny is?"

"My car."

His gaze shifted momentarily from the rearview mirror to her. "You name your car?"

"Doesn't everyone?"

"Not when their car looks as pathetic as yours does."

"Hey, looks aren't everything."

"That's true." He carefully drove around a pair of pot-holes near the parking lot entrance. "The problem is that the car doesn't run very well either."

"I just haven't had time to change the oil and give her a tune up."

"Where did you learn to do that stuff?"

"My brother taught me. He said I was the worst student he'd ever had because I refused to remember all the parts and their names. But somehow I get the job done, even if I refer to certain automotive items as whatchamacallits and thingies instead of belts and spark plugs."

"Which just goes to prove that a thingie by any other name is still . . ."

"A spark plug."

They shared a grin. It struck her how good it was to be this way with him—to tease and talk, to relax. Not easy to do given the fact that he was still minus his T-shirt.

He had one of those washboard stomachs that Cyn was always going on about on some of the cover models of her favorite romance novels. And a nice six-pack. The ab muscles. But he didn't have the kind of body building physique that was over the top.

As they said in the classic *Goldilocks and the Three Bears* story, he was just right.

They pulled in front of the Laundromat a moment later, interrupting her appreciation of his body and his company. He'd piled two heavy baskets on top of one another and carried them in before she'd taken one out of the back seat. "You go on and take care of the stuff that's already inside."

He took that basket from her and still managed to hold the door open for her.

"You can't come in here!" The offended comment came from Mr. Drysdale who ran the Laundromat. He stared at Ben and then pointed to the sign on the wall— No Shirt, No Service.

"He just spilled something on his T-shirt," Ellie explained. "We're going to wash it . . ."

"Rules are rules," Mr. Drysdale maintained. "There's a Gas 'n' Go gas station next door that sells T-shirts."

Ellie was about to protest more on his behalf but his hand on her arm stopped her. "I'll be right back," he promised.

And he was. Wearing a black T-shirt that said NASCAR Fans Do It Faster.

"They're referring to house cleaning," he told her, noticing her interest in his shirt.

"I sincerely doubt that."

Ben loaded two machines with the bedding while she took care of the clothes in two other machines. He watched as she carefully poured some of the perfume-free liquid detergent into each washer before moving on to the next one. He was fascinated by the way she bit her bottom lip right as she measured the clear liquid into the cap. It made him want to kiss her right there in the middle of the Sud-Z Laundromat.

The feeling didn't go away half an hour later as he looked through the glass window of the front loading dryer, watching his old T-shirt rolling around amongst her clothing. Some sort of silky pink camisole kept clinging to his solitary shirt, provocatively wrapping itself around the plain cotton, before playfully falling away.

Okay, now he was sure he had it bad. Thinking her lingerie was seducing his T-shirt in the dryer was a clear sign that he'd lost his mind.

He welcomed the sound of the buzzer on the commercial size dryers indicating that this particular event was over.

But there was more to come as he helped Ellie fold sheets. Not a particularly sexy activity in his experience. But as he was learning every day, anything connected with Ellie was totally unpredictable.

The cotton material was still hot from the dryer as he held two corners while she came closer with her edge of the queen-sized sheet. He was distracted by the lemony scent of her shampoo, by the feel of her fingers brushing against his, by the erotic image of making love to her as she lay naked on this floral sheet. He could almost see her dark hair covering the creamy skin of her bare breasts as she rolled beneath him. . . .

He dropped the sheet.

Ellie grabbed the material before it hit the floor. When she'd asked Ben to help her fold the bedding, she'd never dreamt that it would create such wickedly provocative thoughts. She'd watched his lean fingers hold the floral material and imagined what it would be like to have him in her bed, his folded arms behind his head as he gazed up at her with the sensual promise of things to come. The sheet laying low on his bare hips, well beneath his navel. . . .

She clutched the sheet to her breasts, her heart thumping wildly.

"Sorry about that." Ben's voice was husky. "Let's try it again."

His fingers grazed hers as he struggled to find the two corners he'd held before. His fingers then grazed her breasts. Her startled gaze shot to his.

Was that smoky passion she saw there in his expressive hazel eyes? She licked her lips, a nervous habit. He moved closer, lowering his head, his mouth millimeters away . . .

"You two having a problem over there?" Mr. Drysdale shouted out from the back of the Laundromat.

"No problem," Ellie lied, jumping back. As if having X-Rated fantasies about Ben weren't a problem. Especially given the fact that they'd happened right here in the middle of the Sud-Z Laundromat. Hardly the most romantic place in town, given its flickering fluorescent overhead lights and its constant smell of bleach.

If she could get all hot and bothered about Ben merely by folding a sheet with him, she hated to think what making love with him would be like. Well, actually, she didn't hate thinking about it, she'd been doing that entirely too much lately.

Her first instinct was to back off, to remove herself from his powerful sphere of influence. But Amy adored him, and Ellie couldn't let her weakness hurt her daughter.

So she rolled the now wrinkled sheet into a ball and tossed it in the laundry basket. By the time Ben drove her and the clean laundry home, Ellie had regained her equilibrium.

"Amy has been bugging me for the next installment

of Lady Blush's story. She was so upset that she'd fallen asleep after we got home from miniature golf and dinner and missed you telling her more of the story."

"I was all set to tell her about the dragon named Flamebo."

Ellie cracked up.

"What, you think a dragon named Flamebo is funny? He's got an attitude problem but he's a softie beneath that rough exterior."

"Sounds like someone else I know."

"Me? There's no way I have an attitude problem. Now you . . ."

"Yes?" Her look warned him he was treading on thin ice.

"Look really good today."

"Nice save," she congratulated him.

"I mean it."

"Right."

"I don't say things I don't mean." The intensity of his voice let her know that he wasn't kidding, he wasn't being charming. He was stating a fact. Firmly, emphatically.

"I'll keep that in mind."

"You do that."

"Meanwhile, I was wondering if you'd like to stay for dinner? Amy will be home soon and then afterward you can tell her about Flamebo."

"Sounds like a plan."

Ben helped her make dinner, a simple meal of meat loaf and real mashed potatoes along with fresh zucchini.

After Amy prepared for bed, Ben joined her and Ellie in the bedroom. He sat on the edge of Amy's bed. "Now where were we . . . ?"

"Lady Blush wasn't in the jail," Amy eagerly reminded him. "And maybe there's a dragon."

"Ah yes. Now it comes back to me. . . ."

"Did you forget 'cause you're old?" Amy asked him. "My grandma forgets things because she's old."

Ben shared a rueful look with Ellie. "No, I didn't forget because I'm old. I was just teasing you by pretending to forget. Now back to Lady Blush. Our tough hero Sir Goodknight found the dungeon empty except for a pair of guards. He hid in the shadows and heard one of them talking about how they'd moved Lady Blush the day before."

"Moved her where?"

"To Lord Breedembad's castle."

Ellie's giggle verged on a snort.

"You're making funny noises, Mommy." Amy was not amused.

"Sorry." Ellie tried to look apologetic. "Go on, Ben."

"Well, Breedembad's castle was called All-Moat because it was surrounded by a large moat, making the target just about impossible to attack. And the place was guarded by a mean dragon named Flamebo. But Sir Goodknight refused to give up. He also remembered that All-Moat was rumored to be haunted by a ghost and that gave him an idea. But first he had to deal with that dragon."

Ben paused a moment.

"Go on." Amy nestled into her pillow and hugged the

newly washed Raboo tightly.

"Sir Goodknight made sure that all his men had their combat gear ready, including their helmets. Meanwhile, back at the All-Moat castle, Lady Blush was using her sewing kit to remove a big thorn from the dragon's foot. She and the dragon became friends. She even had a nickname for him. She called him Ernie Infernie instead of Flamebo."

Ellie laughed again and was the recipient of another look from Amy. "Sorry," Ellie murmured.

"The dragon liked Lady Blush because she looked beneath his rough exterior and saw the nice dude he was under all the fire-breathing and roaring. And even though it was difficult for her, the more time she spent with him, the more she came to trust him."

"What about Sir Goodknight?" Amy's sleepy question was spoken around a yawn.

"He was busy planning his rescue of Lady Blush. I'll tell you all about that next time."

"You can kiss me and Raboo good night." She held the toy out to Ben and then threw her arms around him to squeeze him tight as he kissed her cheek.

As Ellie watched the two of them, another chunk of her heart was lost. Once Ben moved away, she tucked the covers around Amy and handed her the freshly washed kitten blanket she nuzzled every night. She kissed her little girl, blinking back the tears at how much she loved her.

Amy patted her cheek. "See you later alligator."

Ellie smiled crookedly. "In a while, crocodile." The silly good-night rhyme ritual was comforting.

She turned out the light and left the door open a bit before joining Ben in the living room.

He looked very serious.

She tried to tease him. "You made Flamebo out to be the hero."

Ben didn't smile. Instead he stunned her by saying, "You were right to turn down my earlier offer to help you. I shouldn't have bluntly offered you money like that."

She blinked, not expecting him to bring that up now. "I appreciate you agreeing with me."

"I'm not agreeing with you. What I'm saying is that I should have offered you marriage."

Chapter Six

"Excuse me?" Ellie was certain she couldn't have heard him correctly.

"I said I should have offered you marriage."

"No way. I mean, that is not a good idea at all."

"Why not? If we were married I'd be even better able to help you look after Amy, to make sure the two of you were taken care of."

"I've already told you, I'm not Lady Blush. I don't need some big knight to come rescue me."

"So you say."

"So I *mean*."

"What's so bad about being rescued?"

"It means you're entirely dependent on someone else for your well-being and you have to trust them to save you."

"So it comes back to trust."

"Look, I know you mean well. And I know that you were a friend of my brother's, a good friend."

Ben didn't know how much of a good friend he was when he ended up getting his buddy killed.

"But I haven't known you that long," Ellie said.

"We can remedy that. It's the perfect solution. If I married you then I could take care of you and Amy. You'd be protected. You'd never have to worry about money again."

"I'd just have to worry about being married."

"What's to worry about?"

"You've obviously never been married," Ellie retorted.

"I'm not like your ex-husband. I'm not going to run out on my responsibilities."

"We aren't your responsibilities, don't you see that?"

But they were. His friend's dying request had been that Ben look out for Ellie and this was the perfect way to do that.

As if reading his mind, she said, "Look, I realize you promised my brother you'd look after us, but I'm sure he didn't mean for you to marry me."

"We'll never know that."

"Well, I know that I don't want to get married."

"Why not?"

"Because I've already been married and it didn't work out."

"Lots of first marriages don't work out. That doesn't mean that people never marry again." He used that voice men used when they felt they were dealing with an illogical woman.

"I'm not people. I'm me."

"And I'm me. Not your scumbag ex-husband. I'm not going to hurt you the way he did."

"I don't even know you."

"What's there to know? You like me, I like you, Amy likes me, I like Amy. End of story."

"Not even close."

"You don't like me?"

"That's irrelevant."

"Not really. Most people about to get married think it's very relevant."

"We are *not* about to get married."

"Meaning you want a longer engagement?"

"Meaning I'm not marrying you."

"Come on, at least give it some thought."

"What's in this deal for you?"

"Excuse me?"

"You heard me, what's in this deal for you?"

"Meaning that I couldn't possibly be doing this out of the kindness of my heart, right? Meaning that I must have some kind of ulterior motive going on here."

"Do you?"

"No." That felt like a lie to Ben. Because he did have a motive she didn't know about, the guilt driving him to make things better for Ellie and Amy. She didn't know the cause of it, didn't even know of its existence. And he planned on keeping it that way. His burden was for him to bear, and him alone.

"You don't want to marry me."

"Funny, I thought I just said I did."

"You're confused."

"Marines don't get confused."

"Look, I know all about the Marine Corps sense of honor and I realize that you think you're honoring my brother by asking me to marry you, but really that's not what he'd want either of us to do."

"So you said before. And as I said, we have no way of knowing that."

"You should marry someone you love."

"What about you?"

Ellie's heart stopped. Was he trying to tell her that he loved her?

"Don't you want to marry someone you love?" he continued.

"Love didn't serve me very well the first time around."

"My point exactly. This time we have something more going for us. A shared goal."

"Which is?"

"To make Amy's life better."

Pride reared its head. "Are you insinuating that my daughter has a bad life now? That I've failed to take proper care of her?"

"I just meant that working together, you and I, we could do more for Amy than you can do alone."

"I prefer working alone."

"I don't understand why you have to be so stubborn."

"Because otherwise you'll run right over me like a tank. And I've had enough of that in my life. I don't appreciate you coming in here and bossing me around, ordering me how to live my life. I've tried to tell you how I feel about this, but you don't listen to what I say. You just keep going on with your mission with blinders on."

"You're the one with blinders on. You're so traumatized by what happened to you in the past that you're willing to risk your future rather than look at the situation rationally or logically."

"I'm not the one being irrational. You are. Proposing marriage to someone you barely know? If that's not irrational then I don't know what is."

"I'll tell you what is. Refusing to take the help that's offered to you, refusing to see past the tip of your own nose to look at the situation logically."

His comments came dangerously close to something her ex-husband might have said, which made her anger flare even hotter. "Well gee, forgive me if I dare to have my own opinion and to voice it. How terrible of me not to fall into line and obey orders. But that's not me and it never will be. So I think it's best if you leave now."

"Oh sure, take the easy way out instead of talking this through."

"You don't want to talk, you want to argue. No, you just want to *order* me to do what you want. That's not going to happen. So you'd better leave. And take this with you."

She tossed him his T-shirt. He grabbed it in time to narrowly miss it hitting him smack in the face. "Fine. Maybe we could use a little time apart. Maybe that will bring you to your senses."

"Don't count on it."

She couldn't slam the door after him for fear of waking her daughter, but boy she sure wanted to.

What had Ben been thinking? Was he crazy proposing marriage that way? Ellie certainly wasn't looking for another husband. Her previous one hadn't even bothered to show up at the divorce proceedings. He'd let his attorney speak for him.

No, Ellie certainly wasn't looking to get married again. Doing that would only add to her problems, not lessen them.

Cyn pounced on Ellie the second she stepped into the employee's entrance at the back of Al's Place. "I heard you and Mr. Too Yummy For Words were mixing it up at the Laundromat yesterday."

"You heard wrong," Ellie said curtly, still riled up from her argument with Ben the night before.

"You mean he wasn't half-naked?"

"Of course not!"

"He wasn't missing his T-shirt?"

"Well, yes . . ."

"Because you'd torn it off his sexy body?"

"No. We'd been cleaning . . ."

"Stop right there. A handsome Marine who cleans?" Cyn rolled her eyes and pressed her hands to her chest. "I'm in love."

Ellie was not amused. "Fine, then *you* marry him."

"Marry?" Cyn picked up on that instantly. "He asked you to marry him?"

"What? What's going on back here?" Latesha demanded as she joined them.

"Mr. Too Yummy For Words asked Ellie to marry him," Cyn replied.

"Get out!" Latesha turned to Ellie. "I heard you brought him half-naked to the Laundromat, but I had no idea that wedding bells were in the air."

"They aren't." Ellie's response was emphatic. "I turned him down."

"What?" Latesha's eyes widened. "Are you crazy, girlfriend?"

"I'd be crazy if I'd said yes," Ellie retorted. "Ben feels responsible for me, that's why he asked me to marry him. Because my brother asked him to look after me."

Latesha wasn't giving up that easily. "If there's no chemistry, then what was he doing half-naked at the Laundromat?"

"He spilled soda all over his T-shirt so I offered to wash it."

"Mabel who cashiers at the Gas 'n' Go said she almost had a heart attack when he walked in there all bare-chested and muscular. Said she hated selling him a T-shirt, that it was a downright crime to cover up such a fine specimen. Claimed he had a perfect six-pack. And I'm not talking beer, here, I'm talking about abs." Cyn smacked her lips. "Yes, I heard it was a mighty fine sight. I'm just sorry I missed it. He was helping Ellie with her housecleaning," Cyn added for Latesha's benefit, since she'd missed that part of the story.

"Get out! A hottie like him? Who cleans?" At Cyn's nod, Latesha turned to Ellie. "Why aren't you grabbing him, girl?"

"Because I hardly know him."

"I thought Earl checked him out for you and said he was a good guy. No arrests or stuff like that."

"He feels sorry for me."

Latesha frowned. "Earl?"

"No, Ben. That's why he proposed. Because he promised my brother he'd look out for me," she repeated to make her point.

"So you're saying there's absolutely no chemistry at all between you and Ben?" Latesha returned to her earlier question.

Ellie blushed.

"Aha!" Cyn's grin was triumphant. "I thought so."

Ellie hurriedly tried to recover lost ground. "Chemistry isn't everything."

"Maybe not, but it sure counts for a lot."

They were interrupted by the arrival of their boss.

"You girls got nothing better to do?" JayJay demanded. "Get a move on. Move your butts on out there, I've got customers waiting!" Latesha and Cyn hurried off but Jay-Jay stepped in front of Ellie, preventing her from following them. "Not you. Get in my office. I want to talk to you."

"What about the waiting customers?" There were only two people in the entire place, but Ellie was in no hurry for a one-on-one with JayJay. The slight slur in his voice told her that he'd already started drinking, even though it was still early afternoon.

"If you want to keep your job you better not give me any more lip unless you're French kissin' me."

She reluctantly followed JayJay into his small office.

The place was a mess. But that was normal. He had piles of papers covering his desk, while the walls were covered with naked pinups of busty women from calendars. Since JayJay was a chain-smoker, the room was filled with a blue haze. That, mixed with the powerful scent of his too-generous application of cheap aftershave, combined with the ever-present smell of onions that permeated the place was enough to turn her stomach.

But it was the lascivious look in his eyes that really made her feel ill. She'd managed so far to keep her distance from his roving hands, but she had a sinking feeling her time to avoid his groping was up.

"Sit down."

She shook her head. "That's okay . . ."

"I said, sit down." His voice was harsh.

She sat.

Instead of going to the chair behind his desk, he perched on the corner, effectively pinning her in the straight plastic chair between his open thighs. "Ever since you started working here, you act like you're above everyone else."

"I'm sorry you feel that way." Her voice was ultra-polite.

"I don't think you show me the proper respect you should be showing your boss. A woman like you, dumped by her husband, with a snotty-nosed kid to support, you'd think you'd be more appreciative of the favor I did you by letting you work here." He reached out to wind a strand of her hair around his finger.

Ellie tried not to shudder in revulsion even as she

leaned as far away from him as she could. "I do appreciate this job."

"Then act like it." He grabbed her chin and raised it. "Show me a little appreciation. You're a good-looking woman." He lowered his hand to her shoulder. "You've got assets." His hand moved to cup her breast but she shoved him aside and leapt to her feet.

"This really isn't appropriate, Mr. Lange!"

"You mean because I'm married? Don't worry about it. What the little woman don't know won't hurt her."

"I mean because you're my boss. And this is sexual harassment. It's illegal."

"You think I care? My brother is the police chief. If I say you came on to me, he's going to believe me. So don't try using that high-and-mighty voice with me. I've had it with your uppity ways. The way I see it, you've got a choice here—" he yanked her into his arms "—you can mend your ways and be a lot nicer to Jay-Jay or you can get another job."

Ellie desperately evaded his groping hands and foul-smelling mouth. He held her so tightly that she was sure she'd have bruises. "Let me go!"

"I like a feisty woman," he slurred, his wet lips slobbering across her cheek. His hands had a choke hold on her throat.

She reacted instinctively, instructions from a free self-defense class she'd attended at the local public library coming back to her. She shoved his pinky fingers away from her, before lifting her knee to hit him where he was most vulnerable. Then she stomped down on his foot for good measure.

His howl of outrage was enough to send Earl racing in. "What's going on in here? You okay?" The bartender's worried gaze rested on Ellie.

"What are you looking at her for?" JayJay shouted. "The slut attacked me! I think she broke my fingers. Call the police. I'm going to have her charged with assault."

"I don't think you want to do that," Earl said. "Think how it would look if word got out that you'd been beaten by a girl."

"You're right. I won't press charges. But I am firing you." JayJay pointed at Ellie, his little eyes dark with malevolence. "Grab your stuff and get off the premises immediately."

"Hey, boss . . ."

Earl was about to protest but Ellie put her hand on his arm. "Don't." There was no way she could keep working here after what had just transpired. She'd have to find another job.

She was a survivor. She'd manage. Without a knight charging to her rescue.

"I'm sorry, we're not looking for any additional help at this time."

Ellie had heard the same news, put one way or another, all afternoon as she checked with every restaurant in town. A review of the local newspaper's want-ad section wasn't encouraging either. Everything required experience or an education that she didn't have.

She picked Amy up from Frenchie's a little earlier than usual.

"Everything okay, *ma chère?*"

Ellie waited until Amy was busy gathering up her toys before replying. "JayJay and I had a run-in at work. He fired me."

Frenchie cursed softly in both Spanish and French. "What are you going to do now?"

"Find another job."

But that proved to be easier said than done. To make matters worse, Amy was upset by Ben's absence. "Why can't he tell me my story tonight?" She had her lower lip stuck out, a sure sign that a major pout was imminent.

"Because he's busy tonight."

"Is he coming to tell me my story tomorrow night?"

"I don't think so." Ellie patted the bed. "Come on, I'll read you *Cinderella.*"

"Don't want Cinderella. Want Lady Blush and Flamebo."

"Well, I can tell you about them."

"You don't know the story, only Ben does."

"How about if I draw you a picture of Lady Blush and Flamebo?"

"I want Ben!"

Ellie finally got Amy to settle down, but it took a lot of time and energy. The next two days weren't any better. Ellie had created a storybook of drawings she'd done of Ben's characters. But they didn't replace Ben in Amy's eyes.

Matters went further downhill when Tiny the Toyota sputtered and died. The battery was gone. Wouldn't keep a charge at all.

Ellie didn't have enough money in the bank to pay for a new battery and her credit card was already maxed out. Worry and lack of sleep were making her groggy.

But she couldn't rest. She had to get a job. She'd been making the rounds all week and nothing. If she didn't find something soon, she'd have to apply for unemployment benefits.

To make matters worse, Amy had awakened earlier that morning with a case of the sniffles. She'd been lethargic and crabby all day. Ellie wasn't sure if it was her cold or the fact that Amy was missing Ben.

In the middle of that night, when Ellie first heard the sound, she didn't know where she was for a moment or two. The crick in her neck and the smell of newsprint directly beneath her nose told her she must have fallen asleep while going through the want-ads of other area papers on the kitchen table.

The noise came again. The wheezing cough that every parent of an asthmatic child dreads hearing.

Ellie hurried into Amy's room. Her daughter's sniffles had rapidly progressed into something much more, resulting in a full-blown asthma attack.

When none of the usual treatments worked, Ellie knew what she had to do. She dialed 911.

Twenty minutes later, Ellie was standing at the emergency room desk, filling out forms and trying not to panic at the realization that she had no health insurance since she was unemployed. Their physician was with Amy now, so she was in good hands. But her condition was serious. The ride in the ambulance had been harrowing. Ellie had to be strong for Amy, she had to hide her own fear and instead be bedrock solid for her frightened little girl.

There was nothing worse than seeing your child suffering and not being able to do anything to make it better.

And now here Ellie was, at rock bottom, trying to explain that she had no health insurance and that no, she didn't have any other means to pay for the care Amy was getting. No job, no working car, no foreseeable light at the end of the tunnel.

Ellie was close to collapse as the seriousness of their situation hit home with a vengeance. She'd been going for days on little sleep, worry keeping her awake.

As a kid, Ellie had once been hit in the head with a baseball bat. That's how she felt now. Lightheaded and dizzy, as if all the blood were draining from her body . . .

"Ma'am, are you okay?" the nurse asked, clearly concerned. "You're not going to pass out are you?"

Ellie was hazily aware of a strong arm encircling her, pulling her close to rest against a broad masculine chest. "I've got you now." Ben's deep voice rumbled in her ear, offering instant comfort. "Everything is going to be okay."

"H-how did you know where we were?"

"Frenchie called me. She saw the ambulance, saw them take you and Amy. I'd given her my cell number in case of an emergency."

Ellie knew what she had to do. There were times, and this was one of them, when giving in didn't mean giving up. Sometimes it was the only way to keep going. "If your offer of marriage still stands, my answer is yes."

Chapter Seven

"Are you sure?" Ben cupped the back of her head with his big hand.

Ellie nodded.

"You won't regret it, I promise." Ben's gentle hug was one of tender reassurance. "You're making the right decision."

Ellie couldn't speak. Emotion clogged her throat.

Yes, she was tough, and yes she was independent, but surely it wasn't a crime to lean on someone else for a change?

She closed her eyes for a second and tried to regroup her strength.

As she did so, she vaguely heard Ben informing the nurse that he'd be responsible for any financial costs incurred. Then he gently led her to a quiet corner of the waiting room.

Ellie leapt to her feet as the doctor rejoined them shortly thereafter.

"Amy is doing better," he said. "You can go see her now." It had only been a few minutes, but Ellie felt as if a lifetime had gone by since she'd held her little girl in her arms.

"You go ahead, I'll be waiting right here for you," Ben said.

"Would your name be Ben?" Dr. Roberts asked. "If so, I think it would do Amy good to see you as well.

She was trying to say your name."

"What happened?" Ben asked the doctor as he led them through the mazelike hallways in the E.R. to an examining room.

"This attack was triggered by the congestion of a bad cold. Asthma affects the airways, the tubes through which the air you breathe travels to the air sacs where your blood is oxygenated. Smooth muscles surround those airways and when Amy has an asthma attack, those muscles constrict or spasm, squeezing from the outside. These are involuntary muscles, so it's not a matter of telling someone with asthma to calm down or relax. Medication is required to stop the spasms and free the airways again. Here we are."

Ben saw the little girl, looking so small and frail in the hospital bed, hooked up to an IV and other machines, and his heart just about cracked in two. How had Ellie managed to handle all this on her own?

He felt reassured by the fact that the doctor said Amy would be fine, and the realization that Ellie and Amy wouldn't be on their own any longer. From now on, he'd be looking after them. Whatever it took, he'd do.

Because this woman and her young daughter had marched into his very soul and become a part of him.

"Hey, big brother, remember that favor you owe me?" Ben was on his cell phone. Several days had passed since Ellie had agreed to be his wife. It was time to tell his family.

"No," Striker replied.

"I'm getting married."

"Say that again? We must have one of those static-filled connections because, this is funny, I could have sworn I just heard you say that you're getting married."

"That's right. That's what I said."

"I see." Striker had always had the uncanny ability to stay calm in almost any situation, which was one of the things that had served him so well during his time as a Force Recon Marine. "Have you told Mom and Dad?"

"I thought you could do that."

"You thought wrong."

"Come on, hotshot. You're the one who's good with words. The one who thumbs your nose at Mother Nature, who has a lucky streak a mile wide. Not many guys can brag that they made out with their future wife in a storm cellar while a tornado ripped over their heads. Here today, gone tornado. Isn't that what you say?"

"I may be the one who's good with words, but you're the one who's always fighting for the underdog. Bringing home strays. Is that what you're doing here? Is that why you're marrying this woman? Have you thought this through?"

"I made a promise, Striker. I can't go back on that."

"You're a Marine with money now, Ben. There are women out there more than happy to take advantage of that fact."

"Ellie isn't one of them. She wasn't keen on marrying me at first. I had to convince her. I promised my buddy John as he lay dying in my arms I'd take care of her. I owe him that much."

"So this is all about guilt. Not a good way to start a marriage."

"You've only been married a year and already you're an expert on the institution?"

"It doesn't take an expert to see that you're asking for trouble by marrying someone you don't love and who doesn't love you."

Ben's silence was telling.

"Or is there something more you're not telling me? Have you fallen for this woman?" Striker asked.

"Stop calling her this woman. Her name is Ellie."

"Have you fallen for Ellie?"

"That would not be a wise move."

"Why not?"

Ben loved his brother, but he couldn't confide even in him. He couldn't tell him how badly the guilt ate him up inside. He couldn't tell anyone. They'd dismiss it as survivor guilt, but he knew better. He was the one who relived that night in his nightmares over and over again. "Never mind. I only called you to ask you to help break the news to Mom and Dad. They're gonna ask questions I don't want to answer."

"When are you getting married?"

"We're sort of eloping."

Striker just laughed. "We'll see about that."

Their mother was more direct. "No way!"

"Mom, we want a quiet wedding. . . ."

"Fine. You'll have one. But there's no way I'm not coming to my son's wedding." Ben recognized the steel in his mother's normally soft-spoken voice. Others might be deceived by her sweet demeanor but it camouflaged the fact that she was as tough as nails. Angela King Kozlowski needed to be strong to be a Marine's wife and to raise five sons of her own. Ben and his brothers would walk on hot coals for her.

"We'll be down to North Carolina in two days," Angela said. "Your dad is just itching to try out that new RV of his." A year ago his parents had rented an RV and traveled around the western U.S. They'd enjoyed the experience so much they'd purchased their own vehicle a few months ago. "Now tell me about Ellie. I can't wait to meet this girl who stole my son's heart. Does she love you the way she should?"

Ben didn't know what to say. He didn't want his parents knowing that this was a marriage of convenience, so they wouldn't try and talk him out of it. Not that they could, but he wanted to avoid the hassle. And he didn't want them thinking Ellie had tried to snare him in marriage. So he made it up as he went along. "Ellie is wonderful. She's tough and strong like you. But she's also got a big heart. She loves her daughter and is a super mom. Amy is five, she has asthma, but she's a tough kid."

"It sounds like you've fallen hard for both of them."

"Yeah, I have."

Ben had the sinking feeling that that wasn't a lie.

Ellie wasn't sure when she lost control of the wedding plans to elope and tie the knot as quickly, quietly and inconspicuously as possible. She only knew that the situation was spinning increasingly out of control.

She and Ben had intended to get married at the county

courthouse—a quick, no-frills sort of thing. But Cyn had stopped by this morning to check up on Ellie, who once she'd confessed she'd agreed to marry Ben, was a goner.

"The county courthouse?" Cyn held out her hands as if to ward off the image. "No way! I've got a distant cousin who runs a wedding chapel about an hour north of here. It would be perfect."

"We don't want anything fancy and we want to get married this weekend."

Cyn had phoned her cousin and minutes later the arrangements were already completed. "She had a cancellation for this Saturday, so you're in. It's all set."

Latesha had joined them now and both women were gleefully intent on helping her with her wedding trousseau.

"So we all agree, Latesha and I as bridesmaids will wear purple. And Amy is the flower girl, of course. The wedding chapel provides the music and flowers."

"The wedding is the day after tomorrow. What about a wedding dress?" Latesha asked.

"I don't need a wedding dress. I can use that beige suit I have."

"No way." Cyn looked horrified at the very idea. "You can't wear a suit. It will clash with our bridesmaid's dresses. Latesha and I bought them a year ago at a bridal store clearance sale. I told you we'd find a use for them," she reminded Latesha.

"I have a solution." Frenchie spoke up for the first time since joining them a few minutes ago. "I have a dress that would be perfect. I bought it in Paris many years ago. I'll be right back." A few moments later she returned, and handed Ellie a zippered plastic garment bag. "Go try it on."

"I couldn't."

"You must." Frenchie gently shoved Ellie toward the bedroom. "Go on."

The dress fit her like a dream. It was ivory satin and clung in all the right places. The square neckline was simple but elegant, while the back was low cut.

They knocked on her bedroom door. "Come in."

Latesha, Cyn and Frenchie all tumbled into her room. "Ohhhh, it's perfect."

"Here." Cyn reached into her tote bag to pull out a box filled with jewelry. "I have just the thing. . . ." She selected an amethyst necklace and fastened it around Ellie's neck. "It has matching drop earrings . . ." She handed them to her. "There."

"You look like a medieval princess. Way to go, Frenchie!" Latesha and Cyn both high-fived the older woman. "I do believe Cinderella is ready for her wedding on Saturday."

"Group hug," Latesha announced.

"Don't wrinkle the dress," Cyn warned as they all snuggled for an empowering embrace.

Blinking back tears, Ellie said, "Have I told you guys lately how grateful I am to have incredible friends like you?"

They all stepped back and reached for the box of facial tissues to dab at their damp faces. "Enough weeping," Cyn said. "When is Ben's family coming?"

"They're supposed to be arriving tonight. We're all

having dinner together at the steak house."

"What are his parents like?" Latesha asked.

"Ben says they're very nice."

"Does he have any brothers?" Cyn wanted to know.

Ellie nodded. "Lots of them."

"I suppose they're all married."

"Only one of them is," Ellie assured them. "The other three are still single. They're all Marines."

Cyn grinned and rubbed her hands in anticipation.

"I'm not sure how many of them will be coming to the wedding, though," Ellie added. "They may not be able to get away. I know that Striker is coming, but he's the married brother. Ben thought his brother Rad will be here but he's not sure about the twins."

"Did you hear that, Latesha? Twins. One for me, one for you."

"I've already found me a fine man," Latesha announced.

Cyn's eyebrow raised. "You have? Since when?"

"Since a few days ago."

"Who?"

Latesha blushed. "Earl."

"Interesting. I'll get back to you and Earl later." Cyn's attention returned to Ellie. "Twins run in families you know. Which means you and Ben could have twins."

If their marriage was going to be a normal one, that might be a possibility. But he'd made it clear that this would be a marriage of convenience only.

The conversation had taken place in a deserted waiting room in the hospital shortly after she'd accepted his proposal.

"I want to reassure you that this will be a marriage in name only," he'd said. "I'm not expecting you to share my bed immediately."

Which meant what? she'd worried. That he expected her to share his bed further down the road?

"I don't want you worrying about that. Understand?"

She'd nodded. She could still remember how warm his hands had felt against her cold fingers. Ben was dependable. He had a rock-solid presence.

But she couldn't fall for him. It would be oh-so easy to do so. There was a powerful chemistry between them. Fireworks went off when he kissed her.

But she couldn't lose herself. She had to stay alert, had to protect her heart. Because loving Ben would mean risking everything. Trusting him to take care of her and her daughter's well-being was one thing. Trusting him with her innermost secrets and battered emotions was something else again.

She was already afraid that she was taking advantage of Ben's generous nature; she certainly wasn't going to complicate things by adding love to the mix. She wasn't going to make any demands of him.

On the one hand she was telling herself not to fall in love with him and on the other she was telling herself not to make demands on him. Yeah, that made sense. *Not.*

Which was part of the problem. She felt so mixed-up.

The sound of her friends' excited chatter faded into the background as Ellie told herself she was doing the right thing and to stop worrying about doing the wrong thing, even if it was for all the right reasons.

"I don't want to wear a dress." Amy folded her arms across her chest and displayed her stubborn face as only a five-year-old can. "I want to wear my princess costume."

Amy had bounced back quickly from her asthma attack a week earlier, for which Ellie was infinitely glad. The cold departed as quickly as it had come. It had been virulent while it lasted, though, and Ellie was still extra vigilant of Amy's breathing, monitoring her carefully.

"I look pretty in my princess costume, don't I, Ben?"

Amy wandered over to him, leaning against him and gazing up at him.

"Yes, you do, Lady Amy. You look outstanding."

If Ellie weren't already so frazzled and nervous about meeting Ben's parents, she would have insisted that Amy change. But they were already running late.

Ben had warned Ellie that his parents thought this was a love match. Which was one of the many reasons Ellie was nervous about meeting them. The first time she'd met Perry's mother, the older woman had accused Ellie of stealing her son away. Perry had just grinned and tossed off some mocking comment about loving his favorite women fighting over him. The evening had gone downhill from there.

Ellie could only hope that this evening would not be a case of history repeating itself.

To boost her sagging confidence, she'd worn her one

good dress, a simple design in burgundy with a scooped neckline and a respectable hemline. It wouldn't do to show up in the skimpy tank top and denim miniskirt she'd had to wear to work. She'd taken care with her hair, using the curling iron to create cascading curls that she pinned away from her face with a pair of cloisonné hairclips that Frenchie had given her for Christmas last year. A black velvet ribbon around her neck held a cloisonné heart.

"Mommy looks nice, too, right Ben?"

"She looks outstanding."

The heated look Ben gave her should have reassured her. But all she could think about was his parents and whether they'd notice that her clothes weren't new and up-to-date.

Ben looked great. He was wearing a sport jacket along with a light blue shirt and khaki pants. For the first time, he really looked like a Marine with money.

Her nerves increased so that by the time they arrived at the steak house, Ellie was ready to turn around and head back home.

"Mommy, you're squishing my hand," Amy said as they walked to the entrance.

"Sorry, honey." She loosened her grip.

Ben draped a reassuring arm around Ellie's shoulders. "Relax. They're not going to eat you. They're going to like you."

There wasn't time to say anything else because they were greeted at the door by his parents. His mother had short brown hair and vivid green eyes. His dad had even shorter hair than Ben and a nice smile.

Ellie held out a hand. "It's nice to meet you Mr. and Mrs. Kozlowski."

"Call me Angela." She grasped Ellie's hand and squeezed it gently. "Or Mom if you'd prefer. Ben told me that your parents passed away when you were young. That must have been difficult for you. I'm sorry. And I'm so sorry for the loss of your brother." Angela tugged her close and hugged her. It was a real hug, not the polite kind that didn't mean anything. Ellie blinked away the sudden and unexpected surge of tears. "But you've got a new family now. I realize there's no way that we can be a replacement, but I hope you'll let us into your heart." Angela stepped back to smile at her and then at Amy. "And who is this beautiful princess?"

"I'm Lady Amy and I'm starting kindergarten last year."

"Next year," Ellie corrected her.

"I left my helmet at home," Amy added almost apologetically.

"Ben introduced her to helmets. He's been telling her bedtime stories."

Angela's eyebrows rose. "About Marines in combat?"

"No," Amy corrected her. She bounced forward onto her tiptoes with excitement at being the center of attention. "About Lady Blush and Sir Goodknight."

"And Flamebo the dragon and a villain named Sir Breedembad," Ellie added.

His dad cracked up. His slap on Ben's back was meant to indicate his approval.

Ellie didn't have much experience in the father

department. She'd never known her own father, and Perry's dad had died when Perry was a teenager.

But Stan Kozlowski seemed to go out of his way to make her feel at ease. He wasn't a man who spoke much, but when he did, it mattered. He also had a dry sense of humor, similar to Ben's.

The meal went by quickly and without any disasters, for which Ellie was infinitely grateful. Until Angela joined Ellie in the ladies' room. Then her gratitude turned to uneasiness.

Had Angela only been pretending to be kind while she was in front of the others? Was she going to corner Ellie privately and speak her mind?

Ellie was proud of the fact that her hand remained steady as she faced the large mirror and redid her lip stick.

Angela set her purse down on the counter beside Ellie and got out a lipstick of her own. "I'll confess that even though I trust Ben's judgment because he is an incredibly good judge of character, I was still a little nervous about meeting you," Angela said.

"You were?"

She nodded. "But I feel much better now that I have met you. I have a good feeling about you."

"You do?"

"You sound surprised."

Ellie was. She'd grown accustomed to people jumping to the wrong conclusion about her.

"What did Ben tell you about me?" Had he lied about her? Ellie wondered. Was that why Angela liked her? Was that why she wasn't accusing Ellie of being a gold-digger, marrying Ben for his money?

"He told me that you're wonderful. That you're tough and strong but have a big heart. That you have a stubborn and independent streak. That you're a great mom. That you reminded him of me."

"He said all that?"

Angela nodded. "Yes, he did."

"I don't know what to say."

"You don't have to say anything. Just take care of Ben. He's so good at taking care of others that sometimes we forget that he needs TLC too. You're a mother. You know how you worry about your child."

Ellie nodded.

"Well, that continues even when they're grown up. Not that I'd tell any of my sons that. They think they're invincible. They're Marines. It goes with the turf."

"I know."

"I figured you did."

They shared a smile in the mirror. "Yes, I think you'll do just fine with Ben," Angela said.

"Your son is a very special man," Ellie noted.

"Yeah, I know." Angela beamed with pride before giving Ellie a quick hug. "Now we'd better get back out there before my Marine son and husband have that adorable daughter of yours wearing camouflage to go with that helmet she left at home."

"Isn't this more fun than hosting a rehearsal dinner?" Cyn asked Ellie. "The wedding tomorrow is going to be simple. That rehearsal we had in your apartment worked just fine. Except for Amy tripping and landing on Frenchie's lap. And for Latesha's skipping down the aisle."

"That was for effect. I won't do it tomorrow."

"I'm more worried about what you two are doing tonight," Ellie stated from the passenger seat. "About why you've blindfolded me and won't tell me where we're going." Ellie tugged at the red bandanna Cyn had placed around her eyes.

"Keep your hands off that," Cyn insisted.

"I'm getting car sick," Ellie warned them.

"We're almost there." Latesha pulled her car to a stop. "Don't take off that blindfold yet, though."

"You're not taking me to that male stripper place out near the interstate, right?" Ellie asked for the tenth time.

"Of course not," Cyn assured her.

"No way," Latesha stated.

They led her from the car. "Where are we?"

"Someplace where we can have a good time."

"Okay, now watch your step. Oh, wait, you can't see so you can't watch. Never mind, we've got this all under control." Cyn stood on one side of her and Latesha on the other as they carefully guided her inside. Once there, they said, "Take the blindfold off." When she did, they added, "Tah-dah!"

It took a second for Ellie's eyes to adjust to the bright light ahead of her. Only then did she realize that it was a spotlight aimed at a mostly naked guy gyrating on stage to Rod Stewart's "Do Ya Think I'm Sexy?"

"You told me you weren't taking me to a strip place," Ellie said.

"We lied," Cyn and Latesha said in unison, clearly unrepentant.

"Sit down, you're blocking the view!" a middle-aged woman yelled at them.

"That's Mrs. Aronson, the pharmacist from Discount Drugstore," Ellie said in dismay.

"Come on." Cyn took her by the arm and led her forward. "They're saving us a seat up front."

"Who is?"

"Frenchie and Angela."

"Angela?" Surely not . . .

"Yeah. Your future mother-in-law is quite a lady! You lucked out, girlfriend."

Ellie wanted to crawl under the chairs but heaven only knew what was on the floor of this place. Her friends shoved her down the row smack in front of the stage, past women who were leaning forward to tuck dollar bills into the waistband of the guy's tiny black briefs.

"Sorry," Ellie repeated over and over again.

"There you two are! You missed part of the show," Frenchie told them.

"I thought you were baby-sitting Amy tonight."

"Ben and his dad are doing that."

"But I thought they were at a bachelor party for Ben."

"That was a ruse to get you to agree to come out for your bachelorette party."

"Ben is much too smart to have a bachelor party," Angela added. "But just in case his brothers got any wild ideas of surprising him, he has Amy as his cover." Two of Ben's brothers—Striker and Rad—had arrived in town earlier that day. "They won't do anything with her under his care."

"I'm so sorry you were dragged into this. . . ."

Angela patted her hand reassuringly. "I wasn't dragged into anything. I knew what I was getting into. Just don't tell my husband. He might not understand."

Ellie didn't know what to say or where to look. But as the decibel level of the crowd's cheers rose, she realized that a hunk dressed in a policeman's uniform had come on stage to stare at the crowd with a theatrically stern warning about being too rowdy.

Two seconds later he was yanking off his shirt and pants in one fell swoop.

"Yeah!" Cyn yelled. "I do love a guy out of uniform!"

Chapter Eight

Ellie felt the room shudder and bounce, and momentarily wondered if they were having an earthquake before waking up sufficiently to pry an eye open and blearily stare at her daughter's beaming face.

"Wake up, wake up, Mommy! We's getting married today!"

A look at the radio alarm clock on Ellie's bedside table confirmed that it was barely six in the morning. She groaned and tried to pull the sheet over her head. Thanks to her rowdy friends Cyn and Latesha, Ellie hadn't gotten back until almost two last night.

"Come on, Mommy. Hurry!" Amy tugged the sheet away.

Imagining she smelled coffee, Ellie sat up and

hugged Amy. "Who is this wiggle worm in my bed?"

"I'm not a wiggle worm. I'm Lady Amy."

Unable to resist a moment longer, Ellie followed her nose into the kitchen, where she found a brand-new coffeemaker, coffee already perked and ready to drink, along with a note.

I figure Lady Amy will probably be up with the birds and that you might need a big cup of Joe to get you through the morning so I set the timer to 6:00 a.m.

> Enjoy,
> Your about-to-be-husband, Ben

P.S. The coffeemaker is a wedding present from me.

Ellie eagerly poured herself a big mug, adding milk and sugar just the way she liked it. As she gave Amy a bowl of her favorite cereal for breakfast, Ellie realized yet again she had a lot to be grateful for. Her daughter was responding to treatment after her last attack.

And then there was Ben. How could she not be grateful for Ben? A man who programmed the coffeemaker to make her coffee on her wedding morning? It was real hard not to fall in love with a guy like that.

But she and Ben had an agreement. Their marriage was to be based on practicality, not on romance. Because his parents didn't know that fact, Ellie had had to pretend that she was a regular beaming bride-to-be, overcome by her fiancé's love.

In fact, it was becoming increasingly hard to

remember that her upcoming nuptials weren't the real thing in every way.

Which made her wish that her brother could be here. Not that Ben would be marrying her if Johnny was still alive. Ellie would have done anything for Johnny to be alive today but there was no changing reality. Still . . . She missed him deeply.

She needed to remember not to get too caught up in the whirlwind of today's events. She needed to keep her feet on the ground, and her expectations realistic.

Hard to do once Cyn, Latesha and Frenchie all showed up on her doorstep at eight in the morning. The time flew by in a flurry of activity— fussing with her makeup and her nails.

"I think we should apply purple acrylic nails," Cyn stated.

"I think we should use these with the cute little wedding bell appliqués." Latesha held up the package.

"And I think we should just use some nail polish."

Cyn held up Ellie's hand as if they were Exhibit A. "But your nails lack glamour."

"Fine by me," Ellie said.

Ellie had wanted her hair down around her shoulders but Latesha had convinced her to pin it up with a few tendrils romantically framing her face. Standing before the full-length mirror that Frenchie brought from her apartment, she decided that Latesha was right and told her so.

"Of course I'm right. I'm always right."

"Except when you're wrong," Cyn said.

Latesha waved her words away. "A rare occurrence."

The amethyst necklace and matching drop earrings that Cyn had lent her looked perfect as did the ivory satin dress.

Frenchie put an arm around her. "You look beautiful, *ma chère.* You all look lovely." Her gaze included Cyn and Latesha, who did indeed look great in their matching purple gowns.

"How 'bout me?" Amy demanded, tugging on Frenchie's dress, a swirl of purples, oranges and greens.

"You look the most beautiful of all," Frenchie said.

Amy beamed, adorable in the lilac dress they'd found during a rushed visit to a large chain department store in the mall yesterday morning.

Frenchie clapped her hands. "Okay, now that we're done with the final dress rehearsal, everyone take your dresses off and put your travel clothes on. Be careful not to mess your hair or makeup," she cautioned Ellie. "We'll only have time to put your wedding dress on at the chapel, but there won't be much time for anything else."

Ben's parents picked Ellie and Amy up at ten for the hour drive north. Latesha was driving Cyn and Frenchie up. Ben and his brothers would be waiting for them at the Love Me Dew Wedding Chapel.

At least that was the plan, and Ellie knew how much Marines believed in plans and following them through to the last detail.

"We're lost." Ben glared at his older brother. "I don't believe this. You've gotten us lost in the middle of no place!"

"Calm down," Striker said.

"Calm down? I'm going to be late for my own wedding!"

"When did you turn into such a worrywart?"

"When did you turn into such an idiot?" Ben growled.

"Hey, I'm not the one who said let's take that shortcut," Striker growled.

"Yes, you are."

"Oh, yeah, I guess you're right." Striker grinned. "I guess that dog won't hunt, huh?"

"Enough with your Texas sayings. We've got to get to the Love Me Dew Wedding Chapel."

"And we will. As soon as I can find a place along this narrow country road to turn around."

"You better pray we find a place in the next five minutes or we're getting out and picking this SUV up and turning it around ourselves. I should have driven myself in my Bronco. I never should have allowed you to talk me into going with you."

"Would you two quit shouting up there?" their younger brother Rad complained from the back seat of the rented Lexus. "I'm trying to catch a little shut-eye here."

Ben shot him a narrowed look that would have made most men quake with fear, but then Rad wasn't most men. He was definitely the radical one in the family, the one who went his own way. With his dark hair and eyes, he was very popular with the ladies.

"Go back to sleep, little brother," Striker told Rad. "We have the situation under control up here."

"Liar. How does your wife put up with you?"

"She loves me."

"At least she's smart enough not to drive with you," Ben noted.

"She wanted to be with Mom and Dad in the RV so she could spend some time getting to know your wife-to-be. She had a court case in Family Court so she wasn't able to fly in until late last night."

"Too bad she missed Ellie's bachelorette party last night," Rad drawled. "I heard they visited a male stripper place."

"Who told you that?" Ben demanded in disbelief.

"Mom."

The SUV swerved.

"Mom?" Striker repeated in astonishment.

"Yeah. I overheard her talking about it when she called Ellie this morning. Apparently that was some party the females had last night. I gotta say, I'm really looking forward to meeting this fiancée of yours, Ben."

"I've really been looking forward to meeting you," Kate Kozlowski told Ellie as she sat beside her in the back of the RV. "I'm sorry I wasn't able to join you all earlier, but I had an important case that was going to court and it couldn't be delayed."

"Kate is an attorney who works with Children's Services in San Antonio," Angela said.

Ellie could tell that she was very proud of her daughter-in-law. "I understand you and Striker got married a year ago."

"That's right."

"Did you know him long?"

Kate smiled. "I fell in love with him when I was a teenager."

Great. Kate had known Striker for years before marrying him, not the mere days Ellie had known Ben. Kate was also one of those classy blondes who clearly came from a wealthy background. Totally unlike Ellie.

Why wasn't his mother having a hissy fit, accusing Ellie of being some kind of gold digger after her son's money? What was wrong with Angela?

Sure, she'd said she trusted Ben's judgment, that he was a good judge of character. But didn't she see how out of place Ellie was in this picture? A kid who'd grown up in a series of foster homes, a single mom with one broken marriage behind her already. Why weren't any of them looking at her suspiciously? Stan and Angela were acting like dream in-laws, too good to be true. And Kate, even though she'd just arrived, was also warm and approachable. Why were they making her feel so welcome?

Because they were well-bred and decent. They weren't the kind of people who'd get their lives in such a mess that they were forced into a marriage of convenience to get out of it. They weren't the kind who hurriedly got married at the Love Me Dew Wedding Chapel. They planned weddings in the church they'd attended their entire lives, in front of hundreds of guests.

Sure, Stan might just be a retired Marine, but he possessed a rock-solid presence that indicated this was not a man who messed up. This was a man who had things under control.

Ben had that same kind of presence. He hadn't shown any signs of being nervous at the prospect of marrying her. They hadn't even spent that much time together this past week. Instead of getting to know her future husband better, Ellie had been hijacked by Cyn and Latesha and engulfed in their plans for this wedding.

"We're almost there," Angela announced from the front seat.

Trying to swallow her panic, Ellie swallowed her gum instead and ended up coughing.

"Do you want to hug Raboo?" Amy leaned closer to offer her stuffed animal.

This was why Ellie was marrying Ben today. Because of Amy. To ensure a better life for her daughter. She'd do well to remember that. Hopefully it would prevent her from running out of the chapel. . . .

"I told you we'd get here in plenty of time," Striker told Ben as the two stood at the front of the Love Me Dew Wedding Chapel awaiting the bride. Ben had decided not to wear his dress blues uniform today, fearing it might remind Ellie of John's funeral two months ago. Instead he was wearing a black suit, white shirt and burgundy tie. Striker and Rad were similarly dressed. "You were worried for nothing."

"I don't call five minutes plenty of time. We barely pulled into the parking lot before Ellie did."

"She'll never know that." Striker narrowed his gaze suspiciously. "You're not so jumpy because you're having second thoughts about this wedding, are you?

You're not about to do something you're going to regret, are you?"

Ben glared at his brother. "The only thing I regret is having you almost mess up my wedding."

"Put a sock in it, you two," Rad ordered from beside them. "The show is about to start." Sure enough, the recorded music started playing. "Cute kid. Whose idea was the hard hat?"

"Mine." Ben beamed with pride as Amy confidently walked up to the front row where she grinned and waved at him before sitting beside Frenchie.

Ben barely noticed Cyn and Latesha walking down the aisle. Then the music changed and Ellie appeared. The moment he saw her, he felt as if a hand grenade had gone off in his heart. She was gorgeous. A vision. A sexy goddess.

He shot a guilty look at Amy. He shouldn't be thinking such things about the kid's mother. This was a marriage of convenience, not one of lust. He was about to make a vow to look after her and Amy. That's what this was about. Not about his attraction to Ellie, about his fascination with her mouth, her body, her eyes.

Was Ellie nervous? She looked like she was. She looked like she was pausing, taking slower and slower steps . . .

She wasn't going to back out now, was she?

Then she glanced at her daughter and saw Amy's hard hat and her grin.

Ellie's eyes shot to Ben. Oh yeah, she immediately guessed who was to blame for Amy's fashion faux pas. But the little kid had been so adamant about wanting her "helmet," telling Ben the night before that she wanted to look like a Marine. So he'd sneaked the headgear in as if it were contraband.

But Ellie didn't appear to be angry about it. Instead she seemed to relax. And indeed her fingers didn't tremble one bit as he took her hand in his and faced the minister.

Then Ellie smiled at him and Ben knew everything would be okay.

"It was a lovely wedding," Angela told Ellie at the early dinner reception afterward at the nearby Magnolia Restaurant. Their entire party consisted of eleven people.

"Wasn't that better than sneaking out to the county courthouse one afternoon?" Cyn demanded from across the table. "I know you were afraid that I'd signed you up at some tacky place, but my cousin did a nice job."

"Yes, she did." Despite its name, the wedding chapel had been charming with its white clapboard building and its romantic floral wallpaper. The pews had beautiful silk flower arrangements in shades of lavender, ivory and pink.

"Have you forgiven me for allowing Amy to wear her helmet?" Ben leaned closer to ask Ellie.

She nodded. Ben's hand on her shoulder made her go all warm and gooey inside. She hadn't been able to eat much of the steak dinner. She'd also been distracted by the sight of the gold ring on her finger. Ben had asked her if she had any preferences, or if she'd wanted to select her wedding band. She'd only given him two directives—something plain and not too expensive.

He hadn't exactly followed her advice. The ring held a row of brilliant channel-set diamonds in the wide band. Her eyes were continuously drawn to it.

She was married now. *Married.* She reached for her wineglass and gulped the remaining alcohol.

"We can't boogy until you and Ben do," Latesha said.

Ellie's mental picture of her and Ben boogying together amid tangled satin sheets had her pouring more wine in her glass.

"Yeah, when are you and Ben going to dance together?" Cyn asked.

"Dancing? Right, dancing." Ellie took a nervous sip of her drink. "There's no place to dance here."

"Sure there is. Right over there." Cyn pointed to a small section that had a removable wooden floor placed over it. "Your dance floor."

"They won't be quiet until we do this." Ben stood and held out his hand to her. "Come on. Dance with me."

"There's no music."

A second later the sound of something dreamy and instrumental filled the room.

Knowing further protest was useless, Ellie went into her new husband's arms. "This is the first time we've ever danced together," she noted softly.

Ben had to bend his head to hear her. "So let's make this first time memorable, shall we?"

She nodded.

He gently pulled her closer. The satin of her dress provided little protection against the heated appreciation of his touch. His left hand rested low on her back, his fingers widespread to maximize the area he covered. His thumb was brushing sexy little circles along the delineation zone where the low back of her dress ended and her bare skin began.

"Have I told you how beautiful you look today?"

She shook her head.

"Well, you do. Look beautiful, I mean."

"So do you. Look nice, I mean. Not beautiful, because you're too much of a guy for that. Stop grinning like that, I know I sound incoherent." Her voice reflected her irritation with herself.

"That's not why I was grinning."

"Was it because I'm not much of a dancer?"

"Neither am I. At least I'm not as good as those guys you saw on stage last night."

She stumbled and stepped on his foot. "How did you know about that?"

"My brother Rad overheard my mom talking to Kate."

"Kate knows?" Ellie tried not to blush.

"Yeah, what's wrong with that?"

"She's so classy and together."

"Yeah, my brother used to think so, too. Now that he's married her, he knows better."

"Meaning?"

"Meaning that Kate grew up with lots of money but not a lot of hugs or demonstrations of love from her parents."

"At least she had parents."

"So do you now. My mom meant it when she told you that she wants you to think of them as family now."

"I can't believe how nice they've been to me. Why haven't they cornered me and accused me of being a gold digger after your money?"

"Probably because I told them I was the one who had to talk you into marriage."

"That could have just been a clever ploy on my part."

"Oh, yeah, you're just a study of deceit and duplicity."

"You don't think so?" She wasn't sure whether to be insulted or complimented by his words.

"No, I don't think so. Don't get me wrong. I think you can do really well at hiding your emotions when you want to. Like back at Al's Place, when those guys were giving you a hard time. You may have wanted to dump their drinks over their heads, but you didn't."

"I ended up getting fired anyway."

"You never did tell me what happened there."

She shook her head. It wasn't something she wanted to remember.

"Okay, I won't push it." Ben settled her cheek against his chest. "You don't have to talk about it now if you don't want to. I don't want you doing anything you don't want to."

Which was part of the problem. Ellie wanted to do more and more with and to Ben, things that had everything to do with romance and sex, with wedding nights and honeymoons. But he'd made it clear that wasn't what this marriage was about.

"I don't believe this."

Ben stared at the flashing light of the Wedding Bells

Motel. "They planned this you know."

"So it says in their note."

While Ben and Ellie had been engrossed in one another as they'd danced, the rest of their wedding party had sneaked out the back way. "Don't worry about a thing," Angela had written on the large note she'd left on the table for them. "Frenchie says she'll stay with Amy at Ellie's apartment tonight. Your brothers tell me they've taken care of your honeymoon suite arrangements for the night. And your nice friends said they left a bag packed with your things in the suite. We've all driven back to Pine Hills and will see you there. A limo will pick you up tomorrow. Our best wishes for the first night of the rest of your lives . . . with love, Angela and Stan." A bolder handwriting had added, "Not my idea, so don't blame me, Stan."

An envelope beneath the letter had held a room key to the Red Hot Lovers Suite.

"They've marooned us here," Ben said. "Taken all our transportation. That's why my brother insisted he should drive today. I should have guessed he was up to something."

"They've arranged for a limo to drive us home tomorrow."

"We could get a limo to drive us home tonight."

"And hurt your family's feelings?"

"I'd like to hurt my brothers and I'm not talking about their feelings," Ben muttered. "They like playing practical jokes on me."

"You mean there may be itching powder in the marriage bed or something?"

"I don't think they'd go that far."

"It's getting cold out here. We'd better go inside."

Ben immediately removed his suit jacket and put it around her shoulders. Using the key, he quickly inserted it in the lock and guided her inside. Flicking on the lights, he looked around before laughing.

"I guess they were saving tacky for the honeymoon instead of the wedding," Ben noted.

The decorating style was definitely over the top. A majority of the room was taken up with the huge heart-shaped bed with its red velvet bedspread and leopard print throw pillows. The mirrors on the ceiling reflected everything below, including the lava lamps on the end tables.

"Here's the bag." He handed it to her, but since it hadn't been closed properly, most of the contents fell out onto the bed. He picked up the seductive lace and silk nightgown. "I like your friends."

"Oh yeah? They packed this for you." She held up a pair of black silk boxer shorts with red smiley hearts on it.

"It could have been worse. They could have packed us each thongs."

"They may have," Ellie muttered.

"Edible condoms, chocolate body paint, Aphrodisia body oil."

"Gag gifts." She quickly gathered the loose materials and jammed them back in the soft-sided overnight bag. There were no chairs, so she sat on the bed, only to jump up a second later when it vibrated beneath her bottom.

"You okay?"

She nodded. "I was just worrying about Amy. I didn't get to say good night to her. Maybe I should call. . . ."

"She'd fallen asleep on Frenchie's lap while we were dancing. Frenchie has your cell phone number right?"

Ellie nodded.

"Then if Amy needs anything Frenchie will call."

"She might not want to interrupt us."

"Do you really think Frenchie would put your daughter at risk by not calling?" Ben asked.

"No. Frenchie takes excellent care of Amy. It's just that I haven't been away from her at night except when she's been in the hospital, and even then I spend most of the night in the chair next to the bed."

"I wanted to talk to you about Amy. I guess this is as good a time as any. Let's sit down."

"No, wait."

But he guided her down to perch on the end of the bed then leapt up in surprise. "What the . . . ?"

"Welcome to the Happy Vibrating Bed." She pointed to a sign propped against one of the leopard print pillows along with several chocolate kisses.

"There must be a way to turn it off. If you want to go ahead and change, I'll take care of this."

"Change?"

He nodded. "Unless you planned on sleeping in that dress?"

She shook her head. But she wasn't keen on swapping it for that sexy nightgown her friends had left her, either.

As if reading her thoughts, Ben said, "There's probably one of those thick hotel robes in the bathroom hanging from the back of the door."

Considering the layout of this room, she thought it was more likely that there was a see-through negligee hanging in the bathroom. But she was pleasantly surprised to discover that Ben was right.

The robe covered her and the sexy red nightie with material to spare.

She came out of the bathroom to find that Ben had changed into the silky boxer shorts. "It's gotten real hot in here," he said almost apologetically.

It sure had. She couldn't believe how good he looked. Cyn had been right to nickname him Mr. Too Yummy For Words. He was. His tautly muscled and lean-bodied frame was a wonder . . . from the tantalizing swirl of dark hair that disappeared beneath the waistband of his shorts to the masculinity of his legs. Even his knees looked good.

"Somehow I turned on the Flames of Love Fireplace and I can't locate the switch to turn it off."

While Ben worked on that, Ellie noticed the bottle of champagne chilling. Her mouth was dry, so she undid the foil wrapping and started working on the cork.

"Here, let me do that." Ben took the bottle from her, expertly popped the cork, and poured them both a glass. "To a most memorable wedding night." He took a sip before adding, "I fixed the bed so it should be safe to sit on now. Like I said, I wanted to talk about Amy."

Because Ellie's knees were getting weaker by the minute, she sat, but only after refilling her empty glass with more champagne.

141

Was it her imagination or did Ben look a little nervous? Maybe it was the strange light in here, provided by the red-tinted light bulbs in the overhead chandelier.

"I wanted your thoughts on the idea of my adopting her. I know, I know, she already has a father. But he hasn't shown much interest in her up to this point and I don't see any signs of that changing in the future. As you probably know, Kate is an attorney who deals in family law. Granted she practices in Texas, but I bet she could head us in the right direction, maybe give us a referral to a good attorney here in North Carolina who can handle the adoption process for us."

"I don't know what to say." She could hardly think at all with him sitting half-naked beside her, the Flames of Love flickering in the background.

"Say you'll think about it. I've also been thinking about where we should live. I'll be returning from my leave in a few days and Pine Hills is almost an hour commute to Camp Lejeune. What are your thoughts about moving a little closer? Maybe get a rental house, one with hardwood floors for Amy, one that we could have outfitted the way you want it. I know how much you love your friends and your neighbor Frenchie. If you hate the idea, we can look for a place in Pine Hills. What do you say?"

"What do I say?" Ellie shakenly set her empty champagne glass on the floor. She put her hands on his bare shoulders and tumbled him back onto the bed. "I say kiss me, Ben."

Chapter Nine

Ellie didn't have time to notice the startled look in Ben's beautiful eyes because a second later he was doing just as she'd asked him. He was kissing her.

No, it was more than that. He was possessing her with a driving hunger.

There was no tentative prelude, no tender beginning. Instead there was total and utter passion, complete with all the desperation and exhilaration that came with such raw emotion.

Unabashed desire blended with the alcohol in her bloodstream, adding its powerfully throbbing beat to her body. Ben made her want things she hadn't wanted in years, things she'd vowed never to get mixed up in again.

He nipped softly at her lips, tugging them deftly apart as he deliciously tasted the inner curve of her upper lip with his tongue. She lay atop him, tethered by the strength of his arm around her waist. Somehow her thick robe had come undone, leaving her with only the sexy nightie. Her lower body rested in the cradle of his hips. The close contact left her in no doubt as to the urgency of his needs. She shifted against him, feeling the rub of his bare thighs.

Thrilled by the sensual friction, she ran her fingers over his muscular chest. Their kisses continued in a heated series that never stopped even as their hands were busy exploring, expressing what brought pleasure. He was so solid, so strong. Yet he shuddered beneath her touch as she brushed her fingertips over his nipples.

Growling deep in his throat, Ben flipped her so that she was now beneath him and he was the one seducing her nipples, caressing them with the repetitive brush of his thumbs. The material of her silky nightgown seemed to amplify his touch, adding another element of pleasure. She slid her arms out of the robe, now completely free of its protection.

He rewarded her move by nudging the thin straps of her nightgown aside with his lips. Using his index fingers, he hooked the straps and lowered the material, baring her breasts to the heat of his gaze.

Since having a child, Ellie felt self-conscious about her body. There were stretch marks where there had been none before. But Ben didn't allow any doubts to enter her mind. Instead he adored her, holding her in the palm of his hand, his mouth finding and surrounding the soft swell of her flesh before closing around the rosy peak. His tongue sweetly stroked her with impassioned need.

Ellie embedded her fingers in his hair and arched off the bed. Shooting pinwheels of bliss were triggered deep within her. She was reeling drunkenly in a sensory world where time and prudence no longer mattered, a place where only this wild pleasure was important.

She barely had time to breathe before he repeated his erotic seduction on her other breast, creating the same sensually intimate response as before.

Bathed in a pool of joy, she shifted her hands down his back, beneath the waistband of his silk boxers. She shivered with the exciting realization that she could shatter his composure the same way he'd shattered hers.

Groaning his pleasure, he shifted so they both lay on their sides. Their kissing resumed with a newfound urgency. She took lipfulls of his mouth. He gave erotic thrusts of his tongue.

He reached out to curl his fingers behind her knee, guiding her bended leg up over his hip. The intimacy of their embrace was increased as he surged against her. The high degree of his arousal was unmistakable.

Which is why she was stunned when a second later Ben abruptly severed all contact, rolling off the bed and leaving the room.

Ellie stared at the closed bathroom door in confusion. Had he gone to get protection? The condoms were still in the bag on the floor in here.

Then she heard the sound of the shower going.

Uncertain of what was going on, she pulled her night-gown back in place and put on the robe once again. Suddenly the Flames of Love Fireplace no longer made the room seem hot. Instead she felt chilled.

She felt even colder when Ben came out of the bath-room wrapped in a towel. Despite his sexy attire, he looked so remote. "I'm sorry. None of that should ever have happened. It was a mistake." His voice was curt. "And it won't happen again." His eyes which had only moments before smoldered with passion now smoldered with determination. "We'll chalk it up to too much alcohol." He grabbed his trousers and shirt before heading back to the bathroom to get dressed again.

A mistake. Never should have happened. What did the guy have to say to make it clear to her that he wasn't interested in making love to her? Oh, sure he'd responded when she'd thrown herself at him in what he considered to be a drunken passion.

Only she knew that alcohol wasn't responsible for her actions. Her feelings for Ben were.

But that didn't matter because those feelings clearly weren't returned. He'd told her that he wasn't looking for a normal marriage. He'd even told her that he didn't plan on going to bed with her. They were married in name only and that's the way he wanted it.

Ellie wrapped the thick robe even closer around her before crawling beneath the covers and tugging them up to her ears, until only the top of her head was showing.

Walking out of the bathroom and finding her curled up in the big bed made Ben feel even more of a jerk. He'd seen the pain in her eyes, the confusion, the desire.

He'd felt the same way but there was nothing he could do to change things. He'd promised her a marriage in name only without the pressure of sex.

She hadn't been herself tonight. He'd noticed the unusually high amount of alcohol she'd consumed. Only a scumbag would take advantage of a woman under those circumstances. Especially a woman he cared deeply about.

So Ben had done the honorable thing. As difficult as it had been, he'd broken off their heated embrace, not wanting to take advantage of her. His body still hadn't recovered, despite the world's longest cold shower that he'd taken.

His remorseful gaze returned to her huddled form. So much for promising to take care of her, for promising not to hurt her.

An instant later she'd tossed the covers off and sat up to glare at him. "I can't breathe that way. And I'm not the kind of woman who hides from her mistakes. So what's next?"

She had just stolen another piece of his heart. This was his Ellie, the one who boldly stood her ground. She was no beaten-down victim.

"What's next?" He tried to sound calm. "We go to sleep."

"There's only one bed."

"I realize that. But it should be big enough for both of us. I'll sleep on top of the covers and you can sleep under them. I called the limo and made arrangements for them to pick us up by seven tomorrow morning, so we better get some shut-eye."

"Fine." She lay back down and turned her back on him.

"Good." He stretched out, still dressed in his pants and shirt, on the opposite side of the bed.

Staring at the blobs in the lava lamp on the bedside table, Ben decided this had to be the most G-Rated wedding night that the Red Hot Lover's Suite had ever witnessed.

"Mommy, I missed you!" Amy hugged her tightly.

"I missed you too, sweetie." Ellie hugged her back.

"Raboo missed you, too. And Raboo and I missed Ben."

"I didn't expect you two back so early," Frenchie noted.

Ellie just smiled vaguely without providing an explanation.

"Did you and Frenchie read the storybook I drew for you about Lady Blush?" she asked her daughter.

Amy nodded.

"I didn't realize you'd drawn pictures to go with my stories," Ben said.

"Mommy did it when you were gone those days and didn't come tell me the story. Lady Blush still needs to be rescued."

"Or to rescue herself." This suggestion came from Ellie.

"Or have Flamebo rescue her." This idea was supplied by Amy.

"You'll find out later tonight," Ben said, "when I tell you the next installment in the story."

"What's an instament?" Amy stumbled over the unfamiliar word.

"An installment is a part, like the next part in the story."

"Where are you going to sleep, Ben?" Amy suddenly asked him. "Are you going to sleep with my mommy?"

"Uh, yeah." He couldn't say anything else, not with Frenchie standing right there. He didn't want the entire neighborhood knowing that theirs was a marriage in name only.

"But I still can come jump in your bed when I get scared, right, Mommy?"

"Right."

"Outstanding." Amy beamed at Ben, using his word to show him that she approved.

Ben waited until Frenchie had returned to her own apartment and Amy was taking a much needed nap later that afternoon before bringing up the matter of sleeping arrangements again. "Have you thought more about what I said last night?"

"About not repeating the mistake of my throwing myself at you?" Ellie countered, misunderstanding him. "Message heard loud and clear. Don't worry. As you said, it won't happen again."

"That's not what I meant."

"That's what you said."

"I never meant to upset you or hurt you."

"I know that. It was my fault. You made it clear what kind of marriage this would be."

"I thought that's the kind of marriage that you wanted."

"Isn't it what you wanted, too?" Ellie countered.

"I want what you want." Ben heard himself talking in circles and became even more frustrated. He couldn't say what he wanted, because even hoping for happiness with Ellie seemed like a betrayal to his buddy John.

Ben had spent months slamming the hatch on the dark secret he harbored and his guilt but it still remained—festering inside him, keeping him awake nights, giving him nightmares about the last moments of John's life.

149

Ben knew he should tell Ellie, he should confess everything to her.

But doing so would probably mean losing her. And he couldn't bear that. So he stumbled along as best he could, not telling her his secrets, not sharing his desires.

Except for last night, their honeymoon night, when his needs had temporarily overcome his better judgment.

Difficult though it had been, he'd broken off their embrace because he was trying to do the right thing by Ellie, to honor his promise of a marriage in name only. He hated the fact that he'd weakened and given in to the passion brewing between them. He was not a man who broke promises. *Ever.*

And in Ellie's case his promises were not just to his buddy John but also to Ellie. He'd promised to look after her, and that he wouldn't coerce her into his bed.

Ellie had been clear about her feelings regarding marriage from day one. She hadn't wanted a husband. No way, no how.

Ben was no fool. He knew she'd only said yes because of Amy.

Which was why he had to stay focused here, and not be distracted by Ellie's lush lips and the memory of them traveling over his bare body. He couldn't afford a repeat of what had happened last night.

"Have you given any more thought to the possibility of moving?" he asked. "I can sleep out here on the couch for a while but . . . ."

"That's not a permanent solution. I suppose the best thing would be . . ." She looked at him.

"Yes? The best thing would be . . . ?" For one brief wild moment Ben wondered if she were going to invite him into her bed. This despite the fact that he'd just had a fierce self-lecture about keeping their relationship platonic. He hated not being in control of his emotions.

"To contact a Realtor about finding us a larger place. My lease here is up next month so I'd better get a move on. No pun intended. I'll call someone tomorrow."

"Right." Ben nodded. "That would be the logical thing to do."

"And we both agree that we want to be logical, right?"

"Right."

Ben was still trying to convince himself of the advantages of logic when he sat down on Amy's bed to tell her another bedtime story starring Lady Blush and Sir Goodknight.

Amy looked so adorable, wearing her pink cat pj's and hugging Raboo, her big brown eyes gazing up at him with adoration. His throat tightened. He didn't deserve this.

"Look at the pictures Mommy drawed." Amy sat up to shove the handmade storybook at him. A series of pencil sketches had been placed in a three-ring binder. The last one showed a castle along with Lady Blush and Flamebo the dragon in the background.

"These are good."

Ellie blushed. "Thanks. They're just rough drawings, anyone could have done them."

"I couldn't."

"Well, I couldn't have come up with the characters

you have. So I guess that makes us a good pair."

"Yeah."

"What's Lady Blush doing now?" Amy demanded.

"Do you remember where she was when we left her?" Ben asked.

Amy nodded. "She was having a tea party with Flamebo."

Ellie frowned. "I must have missed that."

Ben explained, "It was the night you had your bachelorette celebration and I baby-sat Amy."

"Right."

"The day after the tea party, a guard at the All-Moat Castle noticed a group of people approaching. As they got closer, he realized that they were monks leading a donkey. They told the guard that they'd come to rid the castle of its ghost. The lead monk identified himself as Friar Tankard and his assistant as Friar Stein."

Ellie grinned.

Ben noticed how he'd grown to watch her expressions as he did his storytelling. Her reaction provided him with pleasure. So much about her provided him with pleasure. He yanked his thoughts back to his story.

"Sir Badlord and Sir Breedembad approved the plan for the monks to set up their ghost-busting equipment. While everyone in the castle watched the exorcism, Friar Tankard slipped off without being noticed. It turns out he wasn't Friar Tankard at all, but was Sir Good-knight in disguise. When he reached the wine cellar he realized how heavily guarded it still was so he figured that's where they were hiding Lady Blush. The guards refused to leave their posts to go watch the ghost-busting going on upstairs, so GK showed them a strange looking box. When the guards leaned closer to see, they instantly fell to the ground as the chloroform knocked them out."

"What's chlorfim?" Amy struggled over the unknown word.

"Chloroform is a type of gas that puts people into a deep sleep."

"A deep sleep like the mean witch used in *Sleeping Beauty*?" Amy asked.

"I guess," Ben said, no pro on classic fairy tales. He had a hard enough time making up this one of his own. "Only this time it was used for a good cause. Now that the guards no longer posed a threat, GK grabbed the keys and entered the wine cellar. When she saw him, Lady Blush almost fainted with excitement—"

"Excuse me?" Ellie interrupted, clearly not amused. "Lady Blush is not the type who faints."

"Fainting isn't a crime," Ben countered.

"It is in my book." Her gaze informed him that she hadn't forgotten the circumstances of their first meeting.

"This isn't your book," Ben replied. "It's Amy's story."

The little girl nodded. "Right, Mommy. It's my story."

Ellie wasn't about to give up that easily. "It's a story about Lady Blush. Who isn't afraid of a big dragon."

"That's right," Amy agreed.

"And is therefore not the fainting kind," Ellie concluded triumphantly.

Ben rolled his eyes. "Okay, fine. GK enters the wine cellar and Lady Blush—"

"Is waiting there with Flamebo," Ellie interrupted him, her voice alive with the excitement of one who has just had a creative lightbulb moment. "Who has now befriended her and is ready to protect her. Not knowing who GK is, the dragon is ready to breathe fire and burn GK to a crisp when Lady Blush intervenes, saving Sir Goodknight's life!"

"Wait a minute here!" Ben protested. "She's not supposed to be saving the hero."

"Why not?"

"Because it's *his* job to save *her.*"

They were clearly no longer talking about the make-believe story here. These were issues that were relevant to their own relationship.

"Maybe she doesn't like sitting around, powerless to do anything to help herself."

"And maybe he doesn't like being made to feel like he's not needed."

"Maybe Flamebo saved them both," Amy suggested. "He's not such a mean dragon after all, is he?"

"Not with a nickname like Ernie Infernie," Ellie noted.

"So how do Flamebo, Lady Blush and GK escape?" Amy asked. "Does Flamebo fly them out on his back?"

"I guess we'll find out next time," Ben said with a grin.

"Nice move," Ellie congratulated him after they'd tucked Amy in and returned to the living room. "How does that saying go—leave them crying, leave them laughing, leave them wanting more."

"Yeah, that's how it goes."

Ellie realized the same saying could apply to her relationship with Ben. He'd made her laugh, and he had the power to make her cry. And most of all, he had the ability to make her want more.

"I think this next place may be exactly what you're looking for," their Realtor, Michelle Burbank, told Ellie a week later.

"I sure hope so."

Michelle had the kind of can-do enthusiasm that made her a joy to work with. She'd made the process as painless as possible, but still Ellie was eager to find a new place. Ben had spent his nights sleeping on the couch, getting up before Amy woke so she wouldn't know the unusual sleeping arrangements. It hadn't been easy on him. Or on Ellie.

She'd hear him tossing and turning in the living room and wish she could do something about it. Then her dreams inevitably turned hot and sexy, leaving her wrestling with her sheets . . . and her unfulfilled passion.

"So what do you think?" Michelle asked.

Ellie's steamy thoughts returned to the present and the house they were touring.

"Hardwood floors like you wanted. It's very clean, as well. And quite light and airy. Freshly painted throughout. It has three bedrooms as you requested." Michelle waved a hand down the hallway. "A nice-sized kitchen, recently upgraded. Bath with ceramic tile floor. Has central air-conditioning. Great location. It's closer to Camp Lejeune, which should cut Ben's commuting time. This area also has great schools. Ben told me that your daughter would be starting kindergarten next year."

"That's right."

"So what do you think?"

"I think this is the place. But I'd like Ben to see it."

Ellie called him on the cell phone he'd bought for her. After she'd given him the factual information about this place, he said, "If you like it and think it will suit what you and Amy need, that's fine by me. I trust you. Go ahead and tell Michelle we'll take it."

His confidence in her warmed Ellie's heart.

Ellie turned to Michelle with a big smile. "We'll take it."

"Great. I'll fill out the paperwork. A Realtor is handling the rental arrangements. The owner loves this place and didn't want to sell. They had to relocate for two years but plan on coming back here, so the lease won't be longer than that. Is that a problem?"

"No." Ellie tried to imagine Ben sleeping in the third bedroom two years from now. For some reason, the vision remained hazy.

"There are several Marine Corps families living in this neighborhood," Michelle told her.

Ellie met some of them a little over a week later when she and Cyn stopped by with some packed boxes and a bunch of cleaning materials. While the house was well maintained, there were still things Ellie wanted to take care of herself.

156

One of the things Ben had taken care of, as a wedding present for her, was Tiny the Toyota. When she'd refused to get a new car, he'd had her faithful car completely repainted, detailed, and most importantly, repaired so that it was practically as good as new.

A woman across the street waved at them as she got her mail from the box by the street. She looked to be in her early thirties and had blond hair and a friendly smile. "Welcome to the neighborhood. My name is Trudy. Rumor has it that you're part of our Marine family."

"That's right. My name is Ellie . . . Kozlowski." Even though she and Ben had been married over two weeks now, she still had to pause a moment before giving her new surname.

"Kozlowski? As in Ben Kozlowski?"

Ellie nodded. "That's right. He's my husband."

"Oh, my! The girls hanging around the officer's club are going to be sad to hear that."

Strange, but Ellie hadn't really considered Ben's romantic history until now. She'd been so busy with her own emotional baggage and her determination not to remarry, that she hadn't thought about his background where women were concerned. Dumb her.

"So Ben's quite the ladies' man, huh? Tell us more," Cyn said before grunting as Ellie jabbed her with her elbow.

"Actually his older brother Striker had more of a reputation as a ladies' man," Trudy said. "And his younger brother Rad is one of those dark mysterious types, you know?"

"Oh, yeah," Cyn said, having met Rad at the wedding.

"Not that Ben ever lacked female companionship. In fact, he has a reputation for saving damsels in distress."

"No kidding. How so?" Cyn asked.

"The sister of one his men had an eating disorder and he got her help. The sister of another one of his men had a drug problem and he got her into a treatment program." Trudy went on to give several other examples.

"I'm sorry to interrupt, but we've got to get to work," Ellie said abruptly. Trudy's stories were making her feel like just another one in a long line of Ben's good causes.

"Sure, I understand. If you need anything, just give a holler."

"Thanks."

Once they were inside, Cyn said, "That woman was a fountain of information about Ben."

"There's a definite pattern of behavior there," Ellie muttered, dumping the cleaning stuff on the empty kitchen counter.

"All of it good, according to Trudy."

"Don't you get it?" Ellie turned to face her in exasperation. "The guy has a reputation for helping the sisters of his Marine buddies. Which makes me just another charity case."

"Excuse me, but I don't see Ben marrying anyone but you."

"You don't understand."

"So explain it to me."

Ellie couldn't. She couldn't even explain it to herself.

She only knew that hearing about Ben's past Good Samaritan activities only reinforced her earlier feeling that she'd taken advantage of him.

She also had the feeling that Ben was regretting their marriage. He was still outwardly the same, but she sensed some sort of inner battle going on within him. She'd asked him several times during the past week if everything was okay and he'd assured her it was.

But she'd caught a lost look in his eyes when he didn't know she was watching him. He seemed to deliberately keep their conversations focused on practical, everyday matters of their move instead of even remotely sharing his thoughts or emotions with her.

Hearing Trudy talk about Ben made Ellie realize how little she knew about him. Sure, she'd met his family and had gotten some idea of his childhood. But he'd never talked to her about his life as a Marine. He'd never even told her how he'd first met her brother.

Instead of sharing their memories of Johnny, they both seemed to avoid mentioning him. Which probably wasn't healthy for either one of them. But Ellie didn't know what else to do. She was taking her cue from Ben.

Maybe it was time that she stopped acting like a princess waiting to be rescued. Maybe it was time she did some rescuing of her own, rather than allowing herself and Ben to remain in this quagmire of uncertainty.

"Earth to Ellie." Cyn waved her hand before Ellie's eyes. "Come in, girlfriend."

"Sorry. I was just thinking."

"About Ben?"

Ellie nodded.

"Newlyweds," Cyn muttered in disgust.

Later that afternoon, Ellie returned to the rental house with another load of boxes, this time mostly of kitchen stuff and linens. Cyn had gone to work, so Ellie was on her own.

Ben had arranged for his brother Rad and a few Marine buddies of theirs to help out over the weekend and move the small amount of furniture that Ellie had at the apartment. The only furniture Ben seemed to own was a king-size bed that he'd had delivered out of storage earlier that afternoon. It was the only thing in the house besides boxes.

Ellie was surprised to see Ben's Bronco in the driveway until she glanced at her watch and realized that it was after six. She'd lost track of time. Frenchie had told her not to worry, that she'd take care of Amy this evening, and would stay at Ellie's apartment so that Amy could sleep in her own bed.

Ellie half expected Ben to come out and do his usual protective-guy thing, and take the plastic box from her hands and carry it in himself. But there was no sign of him.

Maybe he was out back in the yard. He'd gotten that guy-lusting-for-machines look in his eyes when he'd seen the grass back there, muttering something about the horsepower he'd need in a lawn mower. And he'd sounded eager about the prospect.

But that was Ben, always taking care of things, of Amy, of her.

For the past two weeks, Ellie had tried to repay the favor by taking care of Ben. But he'd already mentioned that a Chinese laundry pressed his uniforms so he didn't need her for that. Sure, she cooked for him, but that was no big deal.

Which left her wondering what exactly did she have to contribute to this marriage?

And wondering if that's why his mood had changed since their wedding. Had he realized how unequal this whole arrangement was?

His mom had told her to give him TLC, but how could she do that when he made it clear he wasn't interested in her that way? He didn't want any tender loving care from her.

Yet, late at night when she couldn't sleep, she'd toss and turn in her lonely bed remembering their kisses and embraces. She could have sworn the attraction was on both sides.

But if that were true, then why was he acting so strangely? Why had he pushed her away? It was almost as if he'd gone into some kind of a self-contained routine, putting a wall between them. Yet she sensed something else simmering beneath the surface, something deep and painful, something powerful and passionate.

She should be relieved that he wanted to keep things platonic, instead of trying to decipher the shadows she saw in his eyes. But she worried about him. Lack of sleep had deepened the lines on his face. He'd claimed it was because her couch was so short and that he'd sleep better once they completed the move this weekend.

She sure hoped so. She'd hate to think that she'd made Ben's life miserable. Worrying about that was keeping her up at night.

Once she entered the house, she looked straight ahead down the hallway to Ben's bedroom. The doorway was wide open so she could see that he'd fallen asleep on the huge bed.

She quietly set the box down and tiptoed closer, unable to resist the temptation of checking up on him. He was always up and out before she woke in the morning so she never got to see him this way—vulnerable and at peace.

Only he wasn't at peace. His head thrashed on the pillow, his fingers clenched reflexively.

She knew the signs. He was having a nightmare.

She sat down on the edge of the bed. "Ben? Wake up . . ."

His eyes flew open as he grabbed her and yanked her onto the bed beneath him. He was in military mode—his gaze darting from side to side as if searching for danger.

"It's just me." She kept her voice calm even though her heart was pounding like crazy. "I woke you because you were having a nightmare."

Releasing her, Ben rolled away to sit on the edge of the bed and bury his head in his hands for a moment. Raw adrenaline was still shooting through him, leaving every sense on full alert. Lingering remnants of the nightmare continued to hold him in their grip—the jumbled memories imploding upon him. Every night he relived that moment that had changed his life.

Their unit had come under attack. The sudden burst of unexpected gunfire streaking across the night sky. The flash of live ammunition.

"Stay down!" he'd yelled to his men. "Keep low!"

But John hadn't obeyed those orders. Instead he'd launched himself at Ben, who'd felt his buddy's body jerk as the bullet hit him.

And then the shots stopped as suddenly as they'd started.

Ben felt the warm blood dripping through his fingers. John's blood. He'd frantically tried to stem the flow.

Why? Why? Why?

The moon came out from behind the clouds, allowing Ben to see the look in John's eyes, a look that had said it all. He'd taken the bullet to save Ben's life.

Chapter Ten

"Ben?"

He jerked away from her touch.

Hearing Ellie's indrawn breath, he reluctantly turned to face her. The pain etched on her face almost killed him.

"I'm sorry. I shouldn't have bothered you." She scrambled backward off the bed. "It won't happen again."

"Yes, it will." He blindly reached for her hand, tugging her to his side. "I'm going to have that nightmare again and again."

She sensed he was reaching out to her in his own way. "Are you okay?"

"Sure," he answered automatically. "I'm always okay."

"You don't have to be. You don't always have to be the knight coming to the rescue. Sometimes you can be the one who could use a little help. It wouldn't be a sin, you know."

"Wouldn't it?"

"No." She rubbed her thumb over the back of his hand in a soothing gesture. "Do you want to talk about it?"

"Not really."

"Okay. Keep taking deep breaths. It helps."

"You sound like you're talking to Amy," Ben muttered. He knew he couldn't keep putting this moment off. The time had come.

As if sensing his ambivalence, she urged him on. "Talk to me, Ben. I know something has been terribly wrong. Is it me? Are you regretting marrying me?"

He shot her a startled look. "What would make you think that?"

"A lot of things."

"Like what?"

"Like the fact that you don't want me touching you."

"I want it *too* much," he growled.

"I don't understand."

"I promised you a marriage of convenience. A marriage in name only. And I always keep my promises."

"Is that the reason you pulled away from me on our wedding night?"

"Yes."

She sensed he wasn't being completely honest with

her. "The *only* reason?"

His gaze shifted away. How could he explain to her that he was falling for her, falling in love with her strength and her courage? Yet he knew there was no hope for her to return that love, not when he felt responsible for her beloved brother's death.

"Is it because of what I said about marriage?" she asked him uncertainly.

"It's not about *you*." He couldn't stand the fact that she was blaming herself in any way, shape or form. "It's *my* fault."

"What is?"

"Your brother's death." The words burst from his lips. There. The ugly truth was finally out in the open.

"What are you talking about? You told me you weren't the one who shot my brother."

"I wasn't."

"Then how do you figure you're responsible?"

"I should have watched his back the way he watched mine."

"Is there something you're not telling me?" Ellie asked quietly.

Ben looked away from her compassionate eyes.

"So tell me what it is," she urged him. "Do you feel guilty because you're still alive and John isn't?"

"This isn't survivor guilt." Ben bit the words out.

"Then what is it?"

"Don't you understand? When the shooting started, I ordered everyone to stay down. We were on an overnight training mission in the desert. No live ammunition was supposed to be used that night. But incoming gunfire was flying all over the place. John didn't stay down. He leapt toward me. Don't you get it? Your brother died because he took a shot meant for me."

"You think I don't know my brother? You think I don't know you? If you could have prevented him from getting hit, you'd have risked your own life to do that. Just as he risked his life for you. It's what Marines do. Honor, courage, commitment."

"You don't understand . . ."

She placed her fingers on his lips. "Yeah, I do. I know that neither one of us can bring Johnny back no matter how much we want to." She blinked away the tears. "And I know that he wouldn't want you blaming your-self this way. So let's try and look at this logically, okay?"

His sensual mouth quirked in a pale semblance of his customary smile. "*You're* telling *me* to be logical?"

"Absolutely. You tell me that all the time, so now it's my turn. If the shots were coming out of the darkness, there's no way Johnny could have anticipated that that particular shot was coming your way. You said the gun-fire was flying all over the place. He couldn't know that either one of you would be hit. Have you considered that?"

"Not really, no."

"Well, consider it now. I don't know that he actually planned on taking a bullet meant for you. That it was a premeditated act on his part. That's what's been eating you up inside isn't it? That he died instead of you?"

Unable to speak, Ben nodded.

"Did he tell you that before he died? Did he tell you

he'd taken that bullet for you?"

"No. But I saw it in his eyes. . . ."

"Saw what?"

"That he loved me." Ben's voice cracked.

"Maybe it was out of your hands," she said gently. "Out of both of your hands. Have you ever considered that?"

Ben couldn't believe that instead of blaming him, Ellie was trying to console him. "Why are you acting this way? Why aren't you condemning me, swearing at me, throwing me out of your life?"

"You've condemned yourself long enough, Ben." She cupped his face in her hand, turning his tortured gaze toward her. "I think it's time to forgive yourself."

"Can you forgive me?" His voice was rough with emotion.

"You haven't done anything that needs forgiving, Ben. You didn't fire those weapons, you didn't put my brother in harm's way. You need to believe that."

"Do you believe it?"

"Absolutely. Let me show you how much I believe it." She leaned forward to kiss him. She'd only intended to show him how she felt, not to seduce him. But once his lips met hers, the always-present chemistry between them flared out of control.

Groaning, Ben lowered her onto the bed, possessing her mouth with unmistakable hunger. The intensity of the confessions and emotions they'd just shared was reflected in their embrace. Protective walls were stripped away, barriers broken down, leaving them both with the most basic of truths. Ellie knew this man was meant for her and that she was meant for him.

Once again she'd left her heart open to be wounded, but this time Ben didn't push her away. He welcomed her, openly showing her how much he needed her, how deeply he wanted her. It was apparent in the way his tongue tangled with hers, the way he nibbled on the sweet softness of her lower lip.

One kiss blended into another, increasingly more sensual. His mouth engulfed hers in a turbulent seeking of souls.

She wasn't sure who removed his T-shirt. It may have been her, but she thought he was the one responsible. Or maybe it was a joint operation like the way they'd both unbuttoned her sleeveless shirt.

Ben undid the front fastening of her bra and tossed it aside so that he could concentrate on her bare breasts. He lightly teased the rosy crests with the tip of his thumb, brushing back and forth with tender skill. Murmuring her excitement, Ellie curved her hand behind his neck and guided his mouth to her. He took his time, increasing her anticipation as he licked the hollow at the base of her throat, slowly working his way downward.

When he gilded her nipples with a tongue made warm and wet from their kiss, she arched her back off the bed as waves of bliss washed over her.

He didn't hurry, taking his time with her, noting what gave her pleasure and repeating it until she was shivering with the urgency of her need for him.

She wanted to touch him, to explore and revel in him. She shifted against him, placing a string of kisses up his rib cage to his silky-brown nipples. Wanting to do to him what he'd just done to her, she swirled her tongue over him as her hands slid downward, cupping him through his boxers.

"Are you sure this is what you want?" She felt him trembling as he buried his face in her hair.

"I'm sure *you're* what I want," she whispered against his bare chest.

There was no time for talking after that. In short order, her shorts and underwear were removed along with his boxers. Ben ran his hand up her thighs to the place that ached to be touched. His hand cupped her warm and willing flesh before parting the delicate folds to feel the readiness in her. His rhythmic caress propelled her to a new level of pleasure. Surging vibrations were transmitted from his stroking fingers to her womb until her entire being pulsated.

"Now," she gasped, her fingers gripping his backside.

He settled his body into place. His entry was smooth and sensuous, an erotic rush that was wondrous as the warm velvet length of him slid into her welcoming depths, filling her. With a cry of joy she closed around him, drawing him deeper.

His growl of bliss made her heart shiver. With iron control he prolonged the ultimate delight, the silken friction of his movements urging her on, until she was spiraling upward to the pinnacle of passion, an ecstasy that went beyond sensation. She absorbed him into her very being as she was consumed by the intimate ebb and flow of her climax. Moments later he followed her, his back arching, his face etched with male satisfaction as he shouted her name.

Later, as she lay beside him and listened to his heart-beat, Ellie reflected on what Ben had confessed to her earlier.

She didn't know why her brother had done what he'd done that fateful night. She didn't know if he'd taken a bullet for Ben. She only knew that her instincts told her that Johnny had loved life, and wouldn't throw it away needlessly. A greater force had intervened that night. Both men could just as easily have died in the firestorm, instead of one.

Those same instincts told her that she'd fallen head over heels in love with her husband.

Surprisingly, that was no longer such a scary proposition. Instead it filled her with excitement at the possibilities.

"What are you smiling about?" he murmured.

"You. What are you smiling at?"

"You." His dimples flashed, bracketing his wicked grin as he rolled her atop him. "How late will Frenchie baby-sit Amy?"

"She said we didn't have to hurry."

"Then by all means let's take it slow. . . ." he murmured before making love to her all over again.

"I'm starved," Ellie confessed as she joined Latesha and Cyn four days later at Primo Pasta, an Italian restaurant located midway between Pine Hills and her new house. The weather had turned warm for early April, but the sleeveless pale blue linen shirt and matching skirt she wore kept her cool. In fact the entire spring had been hotter than usual. Or maybe it was Ben's presence in her life that had heated things up.

She smiled at the intimate memories of the past few days. They'd managed to squeeze in some private time during the hectic move from her apartment to the new house and had certainly made good use of that big bed of his. Not that their lovemaking had been confined there. They'd almost drowned in the shower twice.

Ellie blushed just thinking about it. A quick glance at her friends told her they hadn't noticed her momentary lapse.

"I'm surprised one of your cousins doesn't own a restaurant," Latesha teased Cyn. "They seem to own just about everything else, from a video store to a wedding chapel."

"Actually my cousin Vinnie was the one who told me about this place. He wants me to check it out, in case he's interested in expanding his business base to include a restaurant. Meanwhile he's promoted me to associate manager of Vinnie's Videos."

Latesha high-fived her. "Way to go!"

"Congratulations." Ellie hugged Cyn.

"With the pay increase I no longer have to work at Al's Place. So I quit two days ago."

"When I heard that Cyn was leaving, well . . . What was the point in putting up with JayJay's stupidity? Earl and I quit the next day," Latesha told Ellie. "But when the owner heard that all his employees had left en masse, he came in and talked to us. We told him how bad things have been, what a lazy loser JayJay is, how he fired you after coming on to you."

"What did the owner say?"

"Mr. Culligan apologized for JayJay's behavior and then fired him."

Ellie paused, the Italian bread she'd just dipped in the specially prepared olive oil and Parmesan cheese frozen midway to her mouth. "JayJay was fired?"

"Yep. Can you believe it?"

Ellie shook her head.

"But wait, there's more. Guess who Mr. Culligan named as the new manager of Al's Place?"

"You?"

"Me? No way." Latesha laughed. "I don't want the hassle of being a manager. He named Earl."

"That's great!" Ellie had always liked Earl.

"I know. But the thing is that Earl is now my boss and well, we've got this thing going between us. . . ."

"They're a couple," Cyn noted mockingly. "I appear to be surrounded by couples. First you and Ben, now Latesha and Earl."

"Don't say it like you're left all by yourself," Latesha protested. "I happen to know all about that exotic dancer you've been seeing."

Cyn grinned and twirled her straw in her diet soda. Her light lilac nails matched the color of her dress, which was piped in black lace. A large amethyst crystal hung from a thick silver chain around her neck. "As I said at the time, I do love a man out of uniform. Speaking of which, Ellie, you've been beaming since we walked in this place. Come on, talk."

Ellie shrugged and swallowed the delicious bread she'd just eaten before dabbing at her lips. "What can I say? Married life just keeps getting better and better."

"Really? Go on." Latesha nudged her. "Tell us more."

"Suffice it to say that your nickname for Ben was accurate. He is too yummy for words."

"You wicked woman you!" Latesha squealed.

Ellie blinked. "What? What did I say?"

"It's not just what you said, it's the way you said it, and that look in your eyes."

"What look?"

"The look of a woman who vows that her husband is too yummy because she's tasted him herself and has firsthand knowledge of such things."

"Such things?" Ellie repeated.

"Such intimate things. Speaking of which, how did you like that red nightgown I got you for your wedding night? Or more to the point how did Ben like it?"

"Frankly, it didn't look that good on him," Ellie replied with a wicked grin of her own.

Cyn tossed a blue packet of artificial sweetener at her. "You're definitely doing better than the last time I saw you last week when you were angsting about Ben's reputation."

"Ben has a reputation?" Latesha repeated. "This is the first I've heard about it. I thought Earl checked him out with his Marine buddies."

"Ben apparently has something of a reputation for helping damsels in distress which made our friend Ellie here think he'd married her to be nice."

"Are you kidding?" Latesha's eyebrows rose. "The guy has been hot for you since day one, Ellie. Anyone with half a brain could see that."

173

"Except for our Ellie here. So what changed in the past week?" Cyn demanded. "Inquiring minds want to know. Was it that wickedly big asset of his?"

Ellie and Latesha were so stunned they almost snorted the sodas they'd been sipping.

"What?" Cyn gave them a look of innocence. "I was referring to that huge bed he has. I was still there with you when it was delivered, remember? Why? What did you wicked women think I meant?"

Ellie tossed the sweetener packet back at her.

"All right, you two," Latesha kiddingly scolded. "No more playing with your food or they'll toss us out of here. Maybe we should change the subject to a safer topic. How's Amy doing? Is she excited about the move?"

"She's not pleased that Frenchie won't be living right across the hall from us anymore. She's staying with Frenchie today."

"Yeah, but it's not like you're moving out of state or anything. You're only twenty minutes down the road. Ten if you take the Interstate."

"And exceed the speed limit," Latesha added.

"I told you that officer's radar gun was broken. There's no way I was going forty in a twenty mile an hour zone."

They paused as their server brought their food. Cyn had ordered the vegetable lasagna while Ellie had chosen the Cabrese salad with tomatoes and fresh mozzarella in balsamic dressing. Latesha went with eggplant parmigiana.

"Yummy," Cyn noted, closing her eyes in appreciation. "I think we should come here more often."

"Let's make a toast," Latesha said, lifting her ice-filled glass of soda. "To us. May we all find what we're looking for."

"And when we find him, please don't let him already be married," Cyn added.

Ellic laughed, while hugging the silent knowledge that she'd already found what she was looking for and his name was Ben.

"So what's this rumor I heard about you playing with Barbie dolls?" Rad mockingly asked Ben as he joined him at a sports bar near the Marine base.

Ben realized that it was Rad's duty as his brother to give Ben a hard time. The brothers all felt that way about one another. "What are you talking about?"

"You and Barbie dolls. Or maybe it was you and an inflatable doll."

"You're the one in need of that kind of assistance," Ben retorted. "I'm a married man."

"Who plays with dolls."

"It was Amy's doll and what's the big deal? That's old news."

Rad shook his head and shot him a reproachful look. "You're goin' soft, bro."

"I still managed to beat you at darts."

"Only because I let you win."

"Yeah, right." Ben wasn't buying that claim for one minute.

"This is the thanks I get for helping you move last weekend?"

"I fed you two pizzas and half a six-pack of beer. What more do you want?"

"A little appreciation."

"Yeah, right."

"You better watch out, you're starting to sound like Striker."

"He sure took off fast enough after my wedding. Didn't even wait for me to get back from my honeymoon."

"He wasn't sure how you'd take us marooning you at that tacky honeymoon motel. I wasn't, either."

"Is that why our folks decided to hightail it out of town so quickly, too?"

"Dad figured since they were so far south, they might as well drive the RV on down to Texas to visit with Striker and Kate. You heard they're going to have a baby, right?"

"Yeah, Striker called me yesterday and told me he was going to be a dad."

"Did you give him some advice?"

"Me?"

"Yeah, you. You're already a daddy to Amy."

"She's a great kid."

"How is the storytelling going?"

"Talk about a tough crowd." Ben laughed ruefully. "I've gotta tell you, a unit of lean mean Marines has nothing on a stubborn five-year-old." Since the night he and Ellie had gotten back from their honeymoon, Ben had tried to wrap up the story of Lady Blush, GK and Flamebo but Amy had nixed everything he'd come up with. He was starting to suspect she just wanted the story to keep going on forever and ever.

"How are the adoption plans going?" Rad asked.

"So far so good. We've hired an attorney here locally, one that Kate recommended, and are taking the preliminary steps to proceed with the adoption."

"That's good, right?"

Ben nodded and took another sip of his beer.

"So if everything is so great in married-land, why are you sitting here with me instead of at home with your lovely wife and her daughter and her Barbies?"

"Can't a guy have a beer with his brother without there being anything wrong?"

"I don't know. I'm not the married one. You are. So you tell me."

"Things are going too well."

"Excuse me?"

"You heard me," Ben muttered, feeling like an idiot. He knew that since he'd first made love to Ellie things had got both incredibly better and a bit worse for him. The latter was entirely due to the fact that he didn't know how she felt about him. He hoped, he guessed . . . but he didn't know. She hadn't said she loved him. "Things are going too well."

"I didn't know there was such a thing."

"You know when you're on a mission and everything is going like clockwork, but you have this uneasy feeling in your gut that something's about to hit the fan?"

Rad nodded.

"Well, that's what this is like."

"Being married?"

"No. Being married is great. Better than I ever dreamed."

"So what's the problem? You're not still feeling guilty about your buddy's death, are you?"

"Ellie and I worked that out."

"Glad to hear it."

"Yeah." Ben was a Marine and as such talking about his feelings or even displaying them was not done.

Which was why it had been so difficult for him to open up with Ellie.

Rad understood all that. Spilling his guts wasn't his way either. Instead, he clapped Ben on the shoulder in a gesture meant to convey his empathy even if it was cloaked in a jocular male way. "If you need to talk . . ."

"Yeah." Ben cleared his throat. "Thanks."

"I mean it. If you ever need to talk . . ."

"Just call Striker," they said in unison, grinning to hide their discomfort at having revealed too much. "Collect."

"What do you think of your new room?" Ellie asked her daughter. "Do you like it?"

Amy nodded. "It's big. I like the castle you drewed on the shades. Can I go next door and play with Mandy?"

Amy had taken the shy little three-year-old under her wing since moving in, and being the stronger one for a change had given Amy a burst of confidence that made Ellie's heart proud.

"Yeah, sweetie. Mandy and her mom are expecting you." She walked her next door and talked briefly with Mandy's mom before returning home.

Ellie was so happy these days that she was tempted to pinch herself. Finally it seemed like all the bad times were behind her. Sure there were still things to work out, but for the first time in a long time she was optimistic about her future and her dreams to have a family.

The sound of a knock on her front door interrupted her thoughts. Thinking it was Amy, she said, "Did you forget something—"

Her words ended abruptly as she realized who was standing on her doorstep.

"Hi, honey," her ex-husband Perry drawled. "Did you miss me?"

Chapter Eleven

Ellie gripped the door frame with one hand. She wasn't afraid of Perry, she was just stunned to see him after so long. "What are you doing here? How did you find me?"

"Now, honey." His smile was as charming as ever. His face was tanned and he appeared to be in great shape. He was wearing a designer polo shirt that matched the blue of his eyes, and a pair of expensive leather shoes peeked out from the knife-like hem of his khaki pants. "Is that any way to greet your long-lost husband?"

"*Ex*-husband. How did you find me?"

"Aren't you going to invite me in?"

She hesitated. She really wasn't keen on having him invade her space.

"Unless you'd rather we aired our dirty laundry out

here on the front porch where anyone can hear." He turned around and waved at the woman across the way, who'd just gone to get her mail from the mailbox by the street.

Ellie let him in. "What do you want?"

"What makes you think I want anything?" he countered as he strolled into the living room, taking stock of everything with one glance.

"Because you're you."

"Maybe I just wanted to see my daughter after all this time."

Her resentment about his cavalier attitude toward fatherhood bubbled to the surface. "Where have you been? Why didn't you keep in touch with her? It was bad enough that you rarely sent any child-support payments, but to forget your own daughter's birthdays. That stinks!"

Perry shrugged and flashed one of his supposedly endearing grins. "You know I'm no good with dates."

"You're no good, period," she muttered under her breath. He didn't even have the decency to act repentant.

"So where is Amy?"

"She's at a friend's house."

"Good. Then we can talk alone."

Ellie folded her arms across her chest, trying to contain her anger. "You never answered me. How did you find me?"

"You gave your new address to my mom."

"So she *did* know where you've been all this time." Ellie had suspected as much.

"Not all the time, no. But I do check in with her from time to time to see how things are going."

"To borrow money, you mean."

Perry shot her a reproachful look, a lock of his sun-streaked hair tumbling over his forehead. "I'm sensing some hostility on your part. That's a shame. It looks like things have turned out great for you, so you'd think you'd be in a better mood. Nice place you've got here."

"What do you want?"

He grabbed an apple from the bowl on the dining room table. "I can see that life has been looking up for you lately, Ellie, and I'm glad. Real glad. My mom told me you got remarried."

"That's right. And he'll be back any time now, so you'd better get to the point."

"My mom also told me that you married into money."

"Ben is just a Marine."

"A Marine with money. Don't bother lying, Ellie. I checked him out. He inherited several million dollars. Given that fact, I think it's only fair that you share some of your recently acquired good fortune with me."

"Why should I?"

"Because if you don't, I can make life very difficult for you in a wide variety of ways. Starting with Amy's adoption. I could drag that out for years." His voice remained pleasant, which made his threat all the more disturbing.

"Why would you do that? Are you telling me that, after all this time, suddenly you want to be a good father to Amy?"

"This isn't about being a good father."

His words struck her deeply. "You're right. It's not. It's all about you and what you want. The way it always is."

"If you don't give me what I want I can make trouble for you, Ellie. And not just about Amy. Has this new husband of yours told you that he loves you?"

The look on her face said it all.

"Ah, I didn't think so. I've heard he's the Dudley Do-Right kind. Always tells the truth. He can't lie and say he loves you if he doesn't."

In her panicked state of mind Ellie had no doubt that Perry would do as he threatened and make her life miserable any way he could. "What do you want?"

"I already told you. I just want you to share some of your good fortune with me. Give me the money I need and everyone goes away happy. What do you say?"

Ellie suspected that Perry would take pleasure in trying to ruin her newfound happiness with Ben. She knew that Perry would make good on his threats. She also knew firsthand how convincing Perry could be when telling his lies. He was a consummate con man, able to pull the wool over the most experienced person's eyes. He could indeed make the adoption difficult and Amy certainly didn't need that. The little girl needed a reliable father who would always be there for her. She needed Ben.

With that in mind, Ellie was momentarily tempted to give in to Perry's demands. "How much do you need?"

"I think a hundred thousand should do it."

Ellie was momentarily speechless. Had he always been this bad? She hated to think so. There had been a time when he'd had moments of being much better than he was now. But years of self-indulgence had obliterated any sign of good in him obviously, if he was willing to in effect sell his own daughter for one hundred grand.

Where had the man she'd married gone? Sure, he'd had his faults, but he'd also had a few good traits. She was saddened at the realization that the man she'd fallen in love with and had a child with was gone, transformed into someone who'd use his own daughter to get ahead.

If she gave in to him now, he'd only want more next time. And with a guy like Perry, there would always be a next time if he thought you had something he wanted.

"What's wrong? You don't think your happiness is worth that much?" He smiled at her again, his perfect teeth a slash of white in his tanned face. "Of course it is. So what do you say?"

Looking at him, Ellie knew what she had to do. "What do I say? I say forget it."

"You're making a big mistake." His smile had a nasty edge to it now.

"No, I'm not."

"I can make this adoption deal drag on for years."

"You can try, but I have faith in our attorney. Your track record speaks for itself."

"I can turn over a new leaf, tell the court I've seen the error of my ways and that I want to be a good father to Amy."

"Which would be a lie."

Perry shrugged, her accusations rolling off him like

water off a duck. "Doesn't matter. I can convince the court of my sincerity. I'm telling you, Ellie, you'd be wise to listen to this offer of mine. I can make all kinds of trouble for you, not only with Amy's adoption but with that new husband of yours. You know, the one who hasn't said he loves you. I could tell him how you drove me away. . . ."

"You can tell him whatever lies you want, but Ben won't believe you," Ellie said.

"Damn right, I won't believe a no-good con man over the woman I love," Ben said from the doorway.

Ellie barely had time to register the fact that Ben had just declared his love for her for the very first time before he advanced on Perry, who quickly backed up.

"I do believe it's time for you to leave." Ben used that Marine Corps voice of his, the one that demanded instant obedience. "Let me show you the way out."

"Ben . . ." She didn't want him getting into a fight with her ex. That wouldn't help their case for Ben to adopt Amy.

"Don't worry. I've got everything under control."

She sank onto the couch, only now realizing that her knees were shaking. She still couldn't believe Perry had the audacity to come here and demand payment for his daughter. She still couldn't believe he'd shown up at all. Without any indication that he wanted to see his daughter. What he'd wanted to see was a big check with his name written on it.

She nervously wiped her damp palms on her black shorts. Maybe she shouldn't have been so quick to turn down his offer. Had she done the right thing? Had Ben really said he loved her? What was taking him so long? What was he doing out there with Perry?

As if on cue, Ben walked back into the house.

"What happened?" she demanded.

"Perry made me another offer, lowering his price this time."

"What did you say?"

"I told him to get his attorney to put it in writing and send it to our attorney."

"You're going to pay him off?"

"I'm going to make sure that he won't have the opportunity to take advantage of you or Amy ever again by making sure he's out of your lives forever."

"How did you know he was here?"

"Amy told me."

"Amy knew he was here?"

"She saw him through the living room window next door when he first pulled up. She went outside to greet him and heard him talking to you. She didn't like what she heard, so she had Mandy's mom call me."

"Where is she?" Ellie was frantic at the thought that Amy might be faced with the reality of how shallow her biological father really was.

Ben put a hand on her shoulder before sitting down on the couch beside her. "Calm down. She's still over at Mandy's and she's fine."

"She didn't hear Perry demanding money, did she? No, she couldn't have," Ellie muttered, reassuring herself. "The front door was shut."

"So I rush in here only to find that you've taken care of things yourself and didn't need me to save the day."

185

"I don't need you to save me, I just need you to love me," Ellie said.

"And I do." Ben took her hand and raised it to her lips, palm uppermost. "Have I told you yet how very much?"

"No." Her voice was unsteady but her smile was wide. "But feel free to go ahead and give it your best shot."

"Not until you tell me how you feel about me." He held her hand against his face.

"I think I first started falling in love with you when you walked into Al's Place and told that guy to keep his hands off me. I know you kept stealing bigger and bigger pieces of my heart when you made up Amy's bedtime stories for her. But you know when I was a real goner?"

"No, when?"

"When you gave me that coffeemaker and set it up so I'd wake up to coffee on my wedding morning."

He grinned at her, his dimple flashing. "So that's your weakness, huh? I'll have to remember that. And here's something for you to remember. I love you and I always will." He lowered his lips to hers and kissed her.

"I give up!" Ben dramatically declared later that evening as he sat on the edge of Amy's bed.

"Marines don't give up," Amy reminded him.

"I ended the story with Lady Blush and Sir Goodknight flying off on Flamebo's back and you didn't like that. I ended it with Sir Goodknight putting Sir

186

Breedembad in the dungeon and you didn't like that."

"Don't forget the version where an entire unit of Marines overtake the All-Moat castle," Ellie said from the other side of Amy's bed.

"Right." Ben nodded. "I ended it a dozen other ways, and you're not happy with any of them. Maybe I should just let you come up with the ending."

"Okay," Amy immediately said. "I think they say they love each other and they adopt Flamebo and then eat cake and live happily ever after."

"That's it? No big rescues?"

"They already saved each other, Ben." Amy sounded much older than her years.

Ben gave Ellie a wry smile. "Like mother like daughter."

Amy leaned forward. "But you don't just like us, you love us, right, Ben?"

"Right."

She took his hand and placed it in her mother's before putting her little hand on top of their clasped fingers, nodding approvingly. "Outstanding. We're a family now."

"Yeah," Ben agreed, his eyes filled with love. "We're a family."

"So when are we getting a dragon?" Amy asked.

A year later . . .

"Are you ready for your storybook wedding to begin?" Latesha asked Ellie as they stood in the anteroom of the church.

"Actually we're renewing our vows on our first anniversary."

"A brilliant idea," Ellie's sister-in-law Kate congratulated her. "You look absolutely beautiful, by the way. Like Cinderella."

"I'll tell you who looks beautiful. That baby of yours." Kate had had a boy named Sean five months ago.

"Striker and I think so."

"So does Amy. She won't let him out of her sight. She told Ben she wanted us to get a baby next."

"What did Ben say to that?"

"That he was working on it." Ellie's grin reflected her happiness.

"Are you girls good to go in there?" Ben's dad called the question through the closed door. "It's time."

"I think it's so cool that he's walking you down the aisle and giving you away."

"Me, too." Stan and Angela had indeed become real family to her. It might be bending the rules to have her father-in-law walking her down the aisle, but she didn't care. Today was all about celebrating love and she'd grown to love Stan like a father.

Ellie took a last glance in the full-length mirror. Her dress, with its off-the-shoulder bodice over a multi-layered French tulle skirt, was indeed something that would have done Cinderella proud. Dainty horizontal bands of silver glass beads adorned the entire bodice while a seventy-two-inch train trailed royally behind.

Ellie touched her fingers to her reflection as if unable to believe it was really herself she was staring at. Then she carefully turned to face her wedding party—Frenchie as matron of honor, Cyn and Latesha grinning wickedly, and Kate.

"All right, girls, it's time we made our grand entrance. Let's go."

Unlike last time, when Ellie had been so nervous she'd almost run out of the Love Me Dew Wedding Chapel, this time she was utterly confident in her love for Ben and his for her. His adoption of Amy had gone through only a week before, so today was a double celebration.

Amy, now a happy and confident six-year-old, was dressed like a princess and carrying a stuffed dragon named Ernie Infernie along with her basket of flowers. She still loved hearing about the continuing adventures of Lady Blush, Sir Goodknight and the rest of the gang.

Ellie smiled at Stan as she placed her hand on his arm. Then her attention turned to Ben, waiting at the end of the aisle for her along with his groomsmen brothers—Striker, Rad and the twins Steve and Tom. Like Stan, all were dressed in their Marine dress blue uniforms.

The church was filled with friends and family. Ellie didn't get teary eyed until the moment when Amy stepped forward along with Stan to give Ellie into Ben's safekeeping.

"They save each other," Amy told the minister. "And me, too."

At which point Ben just had to pick her up and hug her.

As Ellie renewed her vows to Ben, she marveled at

how her love for him had only increased over the past year. And when the minister finally said, "You may kiss your wife," Ben flashed her a grin that still had the ability to make her heart stop, before kissing her in a way that made her knees weak.

The crowd cheered, the large Marine audience shouting, "Ooh-rah," as they walked back down the aisle and out of the church.

Once outside, they were greeted with six commissioned officers, including all of Ben's brothers. Ben and Ellie paused as Rad issued the command—"Center face." The officers formed two facing lines, three on each side. "Bridge swords." They all raised their swords up to form an arch.

"Ladies and gentlemen, may I present Captain and Mrs. Kozlowski."

As she walked beneath the arch with her husband at her side, Ellie sent a prayer of thanks to her brother, who was with her in spirit.

The reception was held at a country club nearby. Magnolia trees blossomed outside the floor-to-ceiling windows. When Ben and Ellie walked in, the band played the "Marine Corps Hymn." Decorations on the white linen-covered tables included American flags and standards of Ben's Marine Corps unit along with red roses.

Amy claimed her favorite part was when Ben and Ellie cut the wedding cake with Ben's sword. He presented it to Ellie, who cut a slice of the wedding cake with his hand resting over hers.

Latesha maintained that her favorite part was when

she caught the bouquet, only to have Earl propose to her minutes later.

Rad definitely knew what his *least* favorite moment was. He should have seen it coming, but hadn't. All the single Kozlowski brothers had hung back when Ben twirled Ellie's garter around his index finger before pulling it like a slingshot and aiming it directly at his siblings. The twins, Tom and Steve, had instantly ducked. Rad, who'd thought he was safe using his younger brothers as cover, ended up getting hit right between the eyes with the garter.

"I guess we know who's going to be bitten with the marriage bug next," Tom, the more outgoing of the twins, noted with a grin. *"Semper Fidelis!"*

Center Point Publishing
600 Brooks Road ● PO Box 1
Thorndike ME 04986-0001 USA

(207) 568-3717

US & Canada:
1 800 929-9108